BRITAIN AND A SINGLE MARKET EUROPE

WITHDRAWN

Bedford Way Series
Published by Kogan Page in association with the Institute of Education,
University of London

THE BEDFORD WAY SERIES

BRITAIN AND A SINGLE MARKET EUROPE

Prospects for a Common School Curriculum

MARTIN McLEAN

KOGAN PAGE

Published in association with
The Institute of Education, University of London

First published in 1990 by Kogan Page Ltd.,
120 Pentonville Road, London N1 9JN

Typeset by DP Photosetting, Aylesbury, Bucks
Printed and bound in Great Britain by
Biddles Ltd, Guildford

British Library Cataloguing in Publication Data

A CIP catalogue record for this book is available from the British Library

ISBN 0-7494-0098-6

Contents

Preface

When the first draft of this book was completed, the major issue seemed to be the economic unification of western Europe. The creation of a single market in 1992 evoked images of an alternative duomillennium in its expected impact on the economic, social, cultural and educational lives of the peoples of the 12 member states of the European Community. Since then events in the east have given unexpected plausibility to dreams of a Europe from the Atlantic to the Urals. But, in present conditions, books cannot be rewritten as quickly as political systems are changed.

Despite the euphoria, a politically united Europe is still far away. Economic integration looms whether immediately for the twelve or only a little more distantly for the twenty-five or thirty. The examples given in this volume are taken entirely from the 12 member states of the Community. The arguments apply almost equally to the whole of Europe. For it is about the impact of economic union on educational practice. And economic union is not restricted easily to a limited number of European countries.

The removal of economic barriers brings two main consequences for lives of ordinary people and for the schools that serve them. Work moves across national frontiers and so do workers and their families. Schools have to prepare students to compete in a European labour market with their coevals from other countries. Teachers have to be able to meet the needs of migrant children and young people from many European countries.

Economic union is the outcome of political co-operation. But its intention is to encourage competition free from the shelter of national protection. Schools have to be as good as their counterparts elsewhere in Europe if they are not to disadvantage their students. The skilled migrant workers will not be encouraged to move if they feel that their children will be culturally impoverished as a result.

The argument of this work is based upon two propositions. A unified European economy will be based on high technology production. Most workers will be required to think, communicate and act rationally. National education systems which fail to provide opportunities for students to learn to think logically, analytically and schematically may put them at serious disadvantage in a pan-European labour market.

Yet a high technology Europe also has many cultures and sub-cultures. Migrant workers and their families will disperse their cultural aspirations throughout the continent. The second element of the argument is that successful schools will need to be able to respond to an immense diversity of cultural demands which the many peoples of Europe may assert with increasing vigour.

The main chapters deal with the capacity of schools in the present Community countries to meet these twin demands. The focus is upon traditions of valued knowledge and their impact on current practice. The book is concerned ultimately with the ability of the British school system(s) to encourage universally valid rational thought and to accommodate a myriad of European micro-cultures.

English educational culture has become so distanced from the rationalism of continental Europe that it may become a major factor in the social and economic marginalization of British workers in a single market Europe. Moreover, English education has no great tradition of responding to sub-cultural aspirations. However, to minimize the special pleading that often underlies the 'lessons from Europe' approach, the problems faced in other countries are considered first with particular attention to the influential educational cultures of France and West Germany.

My debt to other people is immense. The field is too vast to cover by reading and observation alone and both can be misleading. The richest source has been the interrogative dialogue with many other Europeans which involvement in Comparative Education has brought. Yet this has its limitations. I am aware that the result, despite its criticisms of English education, is still a British view of European culture. But it is a British view which would have been very impoverished had it not been enriched by the patient responses of other Europeans to my questions over several years.

Chapter One
1992 and the School Curriculum

The unification of the content of schooling across the twelve member states is not officially on the agenda of the European Community. There has been a commitment by member governments to maintain the diversity of national educational traditions. This implies that a common curriculum, of all aspects of educational harmonization and co-operation, is the least likely outcome of even the most integrationist schemes of European unification.

Yet protestations of government representatives may not be the most reliable indicators of future change. A pan-European curriculum may emerge from the pressure of localized consumer demand, driven by the logic of European economic union which all the governments are legally committed to achieve by 1992. National governments and the agencies of European regulation may be impelled into facilitating some harmonization of the content of schooling whatever their current views.

However great the pressures for unification, each country has its own traditional and dominant conceptions of what knowledge is of most value. There are points of agreement between these traditions, springing as they do from a common European cultural heritage, but there are major areas of difference. These deeply ingrained ideas are a significant obstacle to curriculum harmonization.

The educational implications of economic unity
What economic changes can force pan-European curriculum unification? They are usually associated with the creation of a unified market in 1992. However, they are broader than that: 1992 simply reinforces existing tendencies towards the reduction of the autonomy and self-sufficiency of national economies.

Multinational companies have become even more important globally since the late 1970s, with international flows of capital, the removal of currency restrictions and the specialization of companies with high capital and technology inputs.[1] Large and complex multinational companies have operations in a range of countries which are mutually interlinked.

Two other developments undermine national economies. First companies which operated exclusively in one country were standard in the first half of this century. Whether private or state controlled they have become significantly less important in recent years. National economies and national economic planning depended on 'national' corporations which are becoming obsolete. Second, specialization has become so acute that small companies operating in a particular sphere in one country are forced to look abroad for larger and co-operative projects. This process was anticipated some time ago in research and teaching in higher education, where cross-national collaboration has provided the only opportunities for the development of knowledge in certain research areas. The same applies to commercial production outside universities and research institutes.

Indeed, there is a view that the nation state with a population of 30 to 60 million which dominated Europe this century is, economically, a temporary phenomenon which was appropriate only to a limited phase in the development of industrialism and capitalism.[2] Such nation states may have predated their economic usefulness and may survive when their economic value has disappeared because they serve cultural and political needs. But the restriction of activity within national state boundaries is no longer a feasible economic strategy except in very large federal systems.

Accompanying these global networks of production and marketing have been labour-flows across countries. Skilled and professional workers need to move from country to country according to the exigencies of production and marketing. International companies have developed procedures by which common selection mechanisms are applied to recruits from different countries. Even without the European single market there would be economic pressures for some harmonization of the content of education across countries to meet the needs of children of highly skilled migrant workers of both multinational companies and smaller-scale specialized businesses.

The unified market of 1992 swims with the tide of the international economy. The original Treaty of Rome of 1957 was based on the principle of freedom of movement in three areas: goods and services; capital; and labour. The impact of this treaty was limited by the persistence of a significant number of non-tariff barriers to free trade, such as the tendency of government agencies to favour national suppliers. The Single European Act, introduced in each country in 1987, attempts to remove practically all existing barriers to the objectives of the Treaty of Rome by 1992. The anticipated economic effects are that cross-border trade will increase so that major companies will market their products in every country; that industrial organizations serving the Community as a whole may be located exclusively in a limited number of regions and countries; and that, as a result, there will be a substantial migration of workers and aspirant workers (including students) across frontiers – most especially of skilled and professional workers.[3]

The broad educational consequences of this economic unification can be plotted. Workers will have to seek jobs in their own specialization in whichever Community country those jobs are available, and they will have to compete with their fellows from other Community states. They will need qualifications acceptable to employers outside their own country and at least as acceptable as those obtainable in other European countries.

Workers will raise families in countries other than their own. Many workers will move from country to country so that their children may have experience of three or four national education systems in the course of a school career. Ease of travel across national boundaries will encourage parents to live in those areas where they can obtain what they believe is the best education for their children even if this is not in the country where the parents work.

Teachers will also become migrant workers, so that some national education systems will have large numbers of foreign teachers. Indeed, this movement may begin before 1992 since a directive of the Council of the European Community of 1988 requires that professional qualifications, including teaching, are mutually recognized and that civil servant status is no longer used to exclude teaching from the terms of the Treaty of Rome.[4]

These developments imply an accommodation between the content and standards of educational qualifications across countries. Curriculum content will need to be harmonized not just at the level of final qualification but at each stage of schooling to allow movement of migrant children. The content of teacher preparation and the content of schooling must be sufficiently common to permit teachers to move across frontiers. Parents, as consumers of the education of their children, will exercise choices which will force schools to compete with their counterparts across frontiers.

Of course, these economic and educational implications of the unified market will depend upon the single economy operating efficiently and equitably. Studies of migrations between European countries after the Treaty of Rome suggest that movement was confined largely to areas such as southern Italy where there were strong 'push' factors for labour migration.[5] Not all remaining barriers will be removed by the implementation of the unified market in 1992. Cultural barriers such as different languages, administrative practices and work behaviour cannot be removed easily.

These obstacles, rather than reducing the need for educational harmonization, will increase the demand for high quality education in disadvantaged areas or for disadvantaged groups so that they can compensate for what they lack in skill and experience in the English language, French administrative practice, German work ethic or Italian style.

Despite the attitudes of the British government, it is unlikely that the European government agencies will be able to avoid the question of harmonization in social policy in the face of these inequalities. Such measures must include at least some aspects of the content of schooling. So examination of pressures for harmonization should include analysis of European Community education policy.

European Community education policy

Community policy on education was ostentatiously unambitious until the late 1980s. The Council of Ministers in a resolution of 1974 rejected the harmonization of national systems of education or policies as a goal in itself.[6] The objectives of the 1976 Community Education Action Programme emphasized projects and the exchange of information on the periphery of educational activity. Yet this tentative strategy has gradually and surreptitiously expanded over time.

At the beginning, educational initiatives of the European Community were limited to areas which directly impinged on the objectives of the Treaty of Rome. Vocational training was one of the few areas of education which was mentioned in this Treaty. Yet from 1963 to 1976 vocational education was handled exclusively by the Social Affairs Directorate of the European Commission which continued to have responsibility for traditional vocational education activities until 1981.[7]

From 1976 the Directorate concerned with education focused on the transition from the school to work, particularly in response to youth unemployment. Yet it did breach the barrier into mainstream education. This provided the opportunity for an eventual redefinition of the educational aspects of vocational training to include the terminal phases of education, including all higher education. It allowed the Commission to become more active in seeking cross-national joint study programmes at higher education level.[8] Mutual recognition of diplomas at higher education level was also agreed in 1985 even though the thorny question of equivalence of content of courses leading to them was not faced.[9] Initial concern for access to vocational training from school had expanded to incorporate European initiatives to harmonize, though by indirect means, the content of the terminal phases of mainstream education.

Another area of Community responsibility identified in 1976 was the education of the children of migrant workers. A directive of 1977 urged governments to allow these children proper access to their language and culture of origin as well as to the language and culture of the host country. Initially it was a peripheral area since migrant workers in the 1970s came largely from poorer countries outside the Community. By the 1980s, however, some of these countries, such as Portugal, Spain and Greece, had joined the European Community while 1992 implies that there will be larger numbers of highly skilled migrant workers from richer Community states. A peripheral policy of the 1970s can then be turned into measures which will enforce a degree of harmonization of content of education in order to give migrant children from major Community countries rights to culture and language similar to those they enjoy in their country of origin.

The 1976 education policy also reflected an older European movement, stressing political and cultural unity, which had preceded the limited economic community established by the Treaty of Rome. The aim was to encourage a European dimension in the content of education in each of the member states. The ideal was ambitious – to remove nationalistic messages from the content of subjects such as history and geography and to encourage recognition of a common European heritage and civilization.[10] The initial measures were very limited – attempts to produce co-operation in limited curriculum projects such as environmental studies for primary schools, the encouragement of international schools which had started before and outside the framework of the European Community and the establishment of institutions such as the European University at Florence. This programme of encouraging European attitudes among young people has continued, especially by facilitating educational exchanges.[11]

Most crucial, however, was the resolution of 1976 that all pupils throughout the Community should have the opportunity to learn at least one other Community language besides their own, together with provision of opportunities for foreign language teachers to visit the countries of the language that they teach. The policy on modern language teaching is fundamental also to the achievement of the Treaty of Rome objective of freedom of movement of labour.

European Community education policy has moved slowly and crabwise. Grand objectives have been proclaimed relating to broad visions of a united Europe or at least an unrestricted common market. They have been followed by actions which, initially, seem paltry and meagre. Small-scale projects have encouraged co-operation between teachers and other educationists across national boundaries and have been sweetened by European Community grants, but by the early 1980s the total achievement of European educational action still seemed minor and diffuse. Nevertheless cumulatively these policies have made possible the major push that has appeared since the mid-1980s. The ERAMUS and COMMET programmes for, first, student exchange at higher education level and, second, for co-operation in science and technology are expanding and encourage the organic evolution of harmonization of the content of schooling.

However, the main achievement of European educational harmonization has come through national policies of each of the member states which are partly the result of European Council of Ministers resolutions but are more usually the outcome of apparently unrelated and independent national political decisions.

The bases of a European curriculum

The construction of a pan-European school curriculum is not primarily a matter for political negotiation at either national or European level. The problem is more fundamental. It involves asking again Herbert Spencer's question, 'What knowledge is most worth?'. Yet philosophical exegesis is not sufficient. The starting point should be what young people need (and want) to know in an economically united Europe.

There is a qualification. Possession of knowledge by itself has little value. Knowledge acquisition is important because of the skills and attitudes which it is hoped it will imbue in students. So worthwhile knowledge has to be defined in terms of the outcomes it has for the behaviour of the recipients (or the benefits the direct consumers believe it will bring to them). Curriculum objectives precede knowledge content.

However the relationship between (behavioural) objectives and knowledge content is quite different in most European cultures from that in North American pragmatic views. The latter assume, in extremis, that purposes should be absolutely supreme and that the appropriate knowledge content can be selected and packaged quite promiscuously to meet these objectives. In western Europe as a whole, the commonly accepted cultural position is that every branch of knowledge has an organic character which can be defined intellectually and which is historically developed. Objectives which define desirable skills and attitudes have to negotiate with the historic intellectual authenticity of each body of knowledge.

It was suggested in the Preface that the prime objective in a European curriculum should be rationality. The argument is that high-technology industry requires its workers at every level to act logically, analytically and systematically. This point can be taken a little further. It is now commonplace to assert that industrial economies have always depended on 'calculative rationality'[12] and, following Max Weber, that states with pluralist, representative governments have a legal-rational basis for legitimacy. The need for rationality is not new. Instead, it is now required by the working, participating population as a whole rather than by minorities, as working practices become more complex and the institutions of pluralist, welfare states become more sophisticated.

In Europe rationality has had a central place in dominant knowledge cultures deriving originally from Plato and Aristotle. There is a view that rationality is not only useful but that it can be individually enhancing and ultimately liberating. This assumption runs through the many attacks on the application of rationality in economic and political spheres, especially the Marxist position that rationality is used to serve class interests and so is distorted into irrationality.[13] But even Marxists hope and believe that a true rationality can be achieved to confront its distorted public version.

The distinction of Jurgen Habermas between 'instrumental mastery' and 'communicative understanding'[14] indicates not only the distance between the actual and the ideal but also a cultural gulf between North America and Europe. American pragmatic 'know how' can become uncomprehending action in the European view. The European ideal of rationality is superior to its uses and allows the individual autonomous control of his or her total world.

European rationalism has also been associated with hierarchies of school subjects. Traditionally, philosophy, mathematics and classical languages were seen to be supremely rational because of their content of logically ordered ideas. Over time, the natural sciences have become increasingly important. But most subjects are capable of a rational treatment – in history, geography and literature, for instance, the emphasis is on synthesis and system building.

This kind of study can defeat its own aims. In practice, the objective of encouraging rational thought can degenerate into the memorizing of large amounts of information. Logical rules and systems can be learned passively without active and creative application. It may deteriorate into little more than a party game – engaging and entertaining in itself but remote from the real world and important issues.

Training in rationality has little place for emotion or for individual and idiosyncratic constructions of the world. It does not engage the economics of human affection. It is public and not private. Yet emotional, individual and private aspirations are important as is the knowledge which can stimulate and sustain them.

It has been suggested that these private knowledge needs are likely to become more important in high-technology economies partly because higher living standards, more education, concentrations of populations in large cities and better communications make it possible for many more people to indulge these aspirations and also for new non-geographical communities of affection and interest to develop.[15] But the survival of these private cultures may also be a protection against the overweening rationality of high technology culture.[16]

Migration encourages the spread of sub-cultures. In a Europe composed of many historic cultures, the movement of peoples will add to existing cultural diversity. National, regional and local school cultures will be challenged by the sub-cultures of economic nomads.[17]

A European curriculum to meet these social and cultural developments would be quite different from that which reflects economic needs. It may include expanded opportunities to study a greater range of languages, religions and historic cultures. But it is more likely to be characterized by the educational capacity to meet the choices of parents and children in the knowledge menus of individual schools or in the organizational structures of local educational institutions and authorities. It will be this ability to meet individual and small community choices for certain kinds of private knowledge while at the same time effectively providing access to rationality-inducing knowledge which will be the measure of effective education in a continent of a myriad of nomadic tribes whose only shared attribute may well be the acceptance of a public rationality.

If then, there, are only two kinds of valid knowledge in an economic

Europe, i.e. rational knowledge and private knowledge, what will be the future position of national knowledge, both historic and pragmatic, and what will be the role of knowledge defined within the other great European tradition of humanism?

National knowledge remains powerful in most countries. It can be separated into two kinds. First, there is the historic knowledge upon which national identities and national political cohesion have been based. It has been treated in curriculum areas such as history, literature and civics. This knowledge has been attacked in the past as anti-European where it encourages intolerance and xenophobia.[18] But new problems emerge when migrants are faced with the national historic knowledge of host communities that do not meet their cultural aspirations and which may be offensive to their own national cultural as well as sub-cultural identities.

There are also pragmatic kinds of national knowledge, especially in areas of morality, social organization, health, political ideology and work. National governments urge that school students should be made aware of certain social and moral issues. There may be a degree of national consensus. But it can break down where there are substantial numbers of migrants in a national system of education. Some conflicts may be related to differing national cultures on, for instance, the relative roles of family and school in areas such as sex education. There may be disputes about the role of school in physical education, sport and leisure. Areas of knowledge which have been seen as part of a pragmatic national curriculum may have to be relegated to the elective private sphere.

A special position may apply to (pre-)vocational education in schools. The assumption made earlier was that universal rational education is also vocational education for most occupations in high-technology industry. Linking the development of rationality with actual experience of work does not violate the rationality principle. But vocational education which socializes children into certain kinds of occupation – especially manual – may also be culturally specific. There are traditions of a work community for which schools can prepare in West Germany which are not paralleled in Britain, France or Spain. Socialization into work communities based on affective relations is part of sub-cultural education rather than universal 'economic' knowledge.

Humanist knowledge presents different kinds of difficulties. It is a historic and pan-European culture which focuses on the moral and aesthetic sensibilities which may be stimulated by contact with literary 'high culture'. In Europe as a whole it has been and still is the culture of

a social élite. In England and Wales there have been attempts to extend
a particular version of humanism to a mass educational market. In this
case it may well become a sub-culture for those parents and students
who wish to avoid an over-concentration on a rational 'high culture' by
emphasizing a humanist alternative. But the position of humanism as
the potential unifying ethos of a European super-élite (as T.S. Eliot
hoped it would remain in England despite the growth of scientific
culture)[19] means that it cannot be regarded simply as a harmless sub-
culture.

These specifications of a potential European curriculum are a
response not only to perceptions of present and future economic and
social change. They should be consistent also with established European epistemological and educational cultures. A new curriculum
should be universal but it should also be European.

Obstacles to curriculum harmonization

Whatever the economic, and less powerfully, political pressures for
harmonization of the content of schooling throughout European
Community countries, there are a number of obstacles to unification.
Differences in the organization/structure of schooling are the most
obvious, though different administrative patterns, in the past the most
serious kind of divergence, are now less significant. The most serious
obstacle, however, is the way that school knowledge is regarded in the
different countries of the Community.

The distinction between centralized and decentralized systems of
education was important in the past. But the major decentralized
system, England and Wales, is becoming as centralized as any other, in
curriculum matters, as a result of the 1988 Education Reform Act.
Ironically, the highly centralized systems of the past, France and Spain,
have permitted greater school-level decision-making on the edges of the
core curriculum in recent years.

The major impact of differing administrative systems is now felt
mainly at regional rather than local levels. Not only does each of the 11
Länder in the Federal Republic of Germany have complete legal
autonomy in educational matters, including school curriculum content,
but there is also important regional or quasi-regional autonomy in
Spain, Belgium, the Netherlands and the United Kingdom. In Belgium
and the Netherlands the *de facto* regionalism is based upon differences
of language (Belgium) or religion (Netherlands). In Britain the regions
are geographically peripheral (Scotland and Northern Ireland). The net
effect is to bring more groups into discussion about harmonization and

thus to increase possibilities of conflict and disagreement.

Differences in structure and organization of schooling are more important. Two kinds of divergence are significant. First, the division between primary and secondary education prevails in every country except Denmark where the 7-16 *folkeskole* provide for compulsory schooling exclusively in one institution.[20] Second, while most European Community countries have common lower secondary education (to ages 15 or 16), differentiated secondary schools based on selection by attainment and different perceived occupational futures of students are still important in the Federal Republic of Germany and the Netherlands. Such differences complicate further any schemes for the prescription of a pan-European curriculum by legislative means.

The most important difference is between residual views of what knowledge is important. This is not simply a question of likely disagreement between professional interests (teachers, academics, employers etc.) in curriculum construction in the various countries or of the concern for the maintenance of national identities among national politicians. It is fundamental divergences in views of what knowledge is most important, how different elements of school knowledge are combined and what broader purposes the transmission of different branches of knowledge serve.

Such divergence does not only threaten the legislative achievement of a European curriculum. It is also an obstacle to the informal movement towards curriculum harmonization, since views of knowledge are entrenched in attitudes throughout education systems and in the cultures in which they are situated. Informal curriculum harmonization under these conditions is likely to produce distortions and inequalities as certain countries, with starkly different approaches to worthwhile knowledge, are left behind in the process of unification which others achieve. In this way national curriculum traditions provide a barrier to European union and penalize those countries which most sharply diverge from their neighbours.

Differences in the content of schooling have been approached by educationists in Europe since the 1960s. The forum has been more often the Council of Europe than the European Community. Projects have involved meetings between teachers, advisers and teacher educators from various countries and the production of synthesized reports of practice.[21] Agreements, where they have occurred, have focused on a shared experience of a movement in some sectors towards pupil-centred pedagogies. The fundamental and residual divergences in traditional philosophies of valued knowledge have not been confronted.

These differences are significant in determining the place and status of different subjects in the school curriculum of the various European countries. They are imprinted into the attitudes of educationists, including teachers in both higher education and schools as well as in other groups in society. Until these differences are overcome, co-operation over the range of content of the school curriculum in the various countries will be difficult to achieve in practice.

Chapter Two
School Knowledge Traditions

The divergence between national views of appropriate school knowledge is not superficially apparent from curriculum content. Primary schools throughout Europe emphasize similar computational and linguistic skills. Secondary schools have the same discrete subjects – language and literature in the national language or mother tongue of students, mathematics, sciences, one or more modern European languages, history, geography, art, music and physical education.

Even within subjects, there is much in common across the countries and not only in areas regarded as 'universal' such as mathematics and science. Literature and history are more specific to national cultures but they have similar kinds of topics – the study of select lists of important books or a chronological treatment of political, economic and social developments within the framework of a common or contingent set of European experiences.

Then communality breaks down. There are quite different expectations of the skills and attitudes that may result from study. There are different hierarchies of status between subjects. Views diverge over what knowledge should be central and compulsory and what can be left to individual choice. Specialization occurs at different times and levels and to different degrees. Within subjects there are often differences between the kind of student cognitive and moral/emotional development that is the hoped-for outcome.

How can these differences be conceptualized in ways that are convincing, rigorous and useful? How can the perils be avoided from the opposite poles of crude and static stereotyping and of patternless complexity? On the one hand, differences should be presented with sufficient lucidity and coherence. On the other, the approach needs to build in possibilities for change within these historical patterns.

Conceptualization of European traditions

Typification of national cultures in Europe has a long history. They became a matter for serious political theorizing in Britain with the rejection of the French revolutionary model of political change by Edmund Burke and others. The point was to make sense of the diverging political processes of Britain and France and to find a rationale for a quite different and distinctive approach in Britain. Similar analysis was encouraged in France by the central place of the revolutionary experience and in Germany and Italy by the nineteenth-century nationalist movement.

Epistemological differences were included in some of these earlier analyses. There was concern in Britain, for instance, about the impact of the 'grand tour' upon the thinking of the social élite in Britain in the early nineteenth century.[1] More systematically, the revival of interest in nationality following the 1919 Versailles political settlement in Europe led to attempts to produce characterizations which included views of worthwhile knowledge. The national character types defined by Salvador de Madariaga – English 'action', French 'thought' and Spanish 'passion' – were extended to consideration of how each type related to thought.[2] The idea was rooted that knowledge and thought had different political and social functions in each national culture.

Comparative educationists gave attention to different epistemological traditions. Joseph Lauwerys characterized the educational knowledge philosophies of the USA, USSR, England, France and (West) Germany.[3] This analysis has considerable value, especially for this study, in its typification of English moral, French rational and German metaphysical traditions. Further analyses have extended the nation-specific approach of Lauwerys by rooting the traditions in philosophical and cultural sources which have influence across countries throughout Europe.[4] Each country has its specific and dominant knowledge tradition which is intelligible throughout Europe because it is also part of a common European culture.

There have been a number of relevant continental European studies which start from intra-national conflicts about what knowledge is most worthwhile. These debates refer back to a pan-European conflict of ideas represented in the educational field by Erasmus and Comenius, the codifiers respectively of the humanist and encyclopaedist educational traditions.

Three traditions may be proposed which are specifically European and are at the same time pan-European:

1. Encyclopaedism
2. Humanism
3. Naturalism

Encyclopaedism and humanism have well established parameters. Naturalism is shorthand for a variety of individual and community orientated views which have challenged the other two dominant traditions.[5]

Yet these views are found in different combinations in the various countries of Europe. Encyclopaedism has been powerful in France since the 1789 revolution and before. Yet it has been very weakly represented in England in the twentieth century. Naturalist views have been more strongly entrenched in England and Germany than in France. Humanism has retained a powerful place in England. Furthermore interpretation varies from country to country and has changed over time. English and German versions of humanism diverge sharply while the French version of encyclopaedism differs from that of Germany.

How can the characteristics of each of these traditions be formulated in ways that will allow them to be used as a tool for investigation of contemporary issues of the school curriculum on a European scale? The types are cultural and sociological as much as philosophical. The need is to establish the parameters of long-established knowledge traditions. The postulations need to be made downstream from philosophy, which transcends national cultures at least in the questions posed, yet upstream from the complexity, confusion and ephemerality of everyday classroom practice.

Description might start from empirical investigation of élite schooling in the first half of the twentieth century – in the French *lycée*, German *Gymnasium*, English grammar or public school and the Italian *licéo*. The assumption is that the curriculum in these schools, on the one hand, reflected more complex configurations in higher education and in the dominant culture. On the other, this curriculum has had a major influence upon lower levels of schooling. Such patterns of curriculum are likely to have survived the democratization of secondary education in the 1960s. They represent a focal point in the whole education and cultural system over a long period of time without, at any time, totally capturing the whole and diverse spectrum of views of worthwhile knowledge prevailing at every level of education or every segment of society.

The starting point is the different dominant views of knowledge in élite secondary education before the main spurt of expanded access occurred in the 1960s. They can be constructed empirically from the statements of the aims of education and the curriculum and from the actual curriculum subjects including their specific content. They can be given greater precision by reference to philosophical, cultural and political positions which justify them.

Encyclopaedism
A definition of encyclopaedism could start from three main principles:

- universality
- rationality
- utility.

Universality has two facets. First, all students should acquire as much knowledge as possible about all valid subjects. All students in countries where the universalist encyclopaedic criterion is accepted have followed the same basic core curriculum even though there may be differences in depth of study between subjects and between students. The second facet is standardization. All state schools offer the same subjects by grade, level and, when limited specialization begins, by broad orientation. Specifications include standard numbers of hours per week and the main aims and topics of each subject.

The universalist principle is now familiar in England and Wales with its adoption in the 1988 Education Reform Act for students up to the age of 16. It has been justified in other European countries on three grounds – that a standard and broad content allows students a width of capacities in later life (including higher study) which early specialization discourages; that it is a form of quality control by which all participants can judge how effectively individual schools and teachers perform against a common standard; and that it goes some way towards guaranteeing at least a limited degree of equality of opportunity through a common experience for all students of whatever backgrounds or perceived abilities.[6]

Yet universalism is the lowest common denominator of encyclopaedism. Its highest aim is rationality. In France, at least, rationalism has been historically linked with the dominant philosophy of René Descartes and with the traditional education developed by the seventeenth-century Jesuits. Since the 1789 Revolution rationality has been regarded as the means to make better people, better society, better government and better economy. At an abstract level it can make better people by imbuing each individual with the light of pure reason which is the highest good and it is the means to understanding the world by the deduction of universal principles of meaning.[7]

How is rationality used to identify central areas and approaches to knowledge? Emile Durkheim contrasted encyclopaedism in French education with humanism by arguing that the former concentrated primarily on nature and the latter on individual man (woman).[8] Yet this rationality did not mean that humanity was ignored. Instead it was studied by reference to universal structures – whether of human relations or the individual psyche. So Durkheim argued that a rationalist, encyclopaedic approach would allow the child to

> understand ideas, customs, political constitutions, forms of domestic organization, ethical and logical systems other than the ones he is used to so that the child will become aware of the vital richness of human nature[9]

in contrast to humanism which was concerned

> with man in all the diverse ways in which he manifests himself through his moral activity as a creature of emotion and will as well as thought.[10]

Durkheim was an encyclopaedist in the sense of believing that all valid knowledge should be imparted. He felt this should be approached through reason and a 'schematic knowledge of each (of the sciences) which covered those ideas most fundamental to them'[11] – repeating Comenius's demand: 'It is the principles, the causes and the uses of all the most important things in existence that we wish all men to learn.'[12] So structure and system created and comprehended by reason were pre-eminent.

The third principle of utility was highlighted after the 1789 Revolution.[13] Rational knowledge is not only valuable for its own sake but for its use. Social, political and economic organizations are made more efficient by the application of rational procedures. Vocational studies, at any level, should begin with rational scientific ideas. A craftsman or woman, a chef who may be an artist as well an artisan, a technician or a professional engineer can all become more efficient by the application of rational scientific principles to practical work. The utility principle means that general academic education is organically linked to vocational studies by the same intellectual principles.[14]

Encyclopaedism is associated with a hierarchy of subjects in the school curriculum. However, it is not simply a system for assigning relative status to these subjects. It affects the selection of topics within subjects, the way they are presented, what is expected of students, their assessment and the way that teachers view themselves. Encyclopaedism can be seen as an ethos running through every aspect of the school curriculum.

Encyclopaedism and the organization of the traditional school curriculum in France

The implications of encyclopaedism for the school curriculum can be judged by confronting first the principles outlined above with the actual organization of the curriculum first in France over the last century.

Despite the claim, considered later, that there has been a movement over time from a universalist to a rationalist orientation, in certain respects universalist principles have been applied more stringently over the course of the twentieth century. In 1900, all students in secondary education followed broadly similar courses in conventional core subjects. The main cleavage was produced by the classics. Until 1902 there was a formal distinction, as in England and Germany, between the classical and modern (or mathematical/scientific) branches of secondary education. The divergence continued informally, based on a division between those taking or not taking Latin, from 1902 through to 1968, when Latin joined Greek as an optional additional subject in lower secondary education.

The provision of universal secondary education in France from 1959 was associated with a renewed application of universalism and standardization rather than with increased diversity. Universalist principles were reinforced by a commitment to achieve equality of opportunity in comprehensive schools through a common curriculum.

Universalism can imply also relative uniformity of student achievement and school quality. This has been central to French conceptions of an encyclopaedic curriculum. All students should acquire a basic knowledge appropriate to their age or grade. Class situated teacher assessment of students has been a perennial feature of French primary and secondary education throughout the twentieth century. So has grade repeating. The principle is that pupils should not move on to a higher level until they have reached a basic prescribed level of achievement for their grade.

Specialization of upper secondary schools potentially has threatened universality. Yet this process has extended the range of options without altering the relationship between a core curriculum and specialisms. In the 1980s there have been five main branches on the general, academic side and a number of others in the technical/vocational section. Yet the core curriculum of French (until the penultimate grade), mathematics, physical and biological science, a modern language, history, geography and civics is still central in all full upper secondary education in France. As with streaming or setting in the lower secondary school, the only concession to differentiation is the pace and depth at which subjects are covered in different branches.

The power of the universalist principle lies in its capacity to survive continuous pressures for differentiation which have been posed by the democratization of lower secondary schooling and the diversification of upper secondary education. It is not simply system inertia but the periodic reaffirmation of communality of educational knowledge in the face of creeping differentiation. Universalism remains central to the ethos of encyclopaedism held by participants in French education.

Rationality is the criterion by which branches of knowledge are recognized to have value in the encyclopaedic tradition. It is the justification for excluding expressive and non-intellectual elements of the curriculum, or more frequently for 'intellectualizing' them. The central place of rationality in secondary schools in nineteenth-century France was expressed in the names of the two alternative final grades of the *lycée – the classe de philosophie* and the *classe de mathématique* – for philosophy and mathematics were seen to be the two supremely rationalist subjects.

Curriculum subjects acquired their rational status in two ways. First, the content of the subjects themselves had to be highly logical and systematic. Second, they had to encourage the development of rational faculties among those who studied them. Some subjects acquired this status more easily than others – not only philosophy and mathematics but also the sciences (especially physical science) and languages (because of their logical structures).

The application of the rationality principle can be gauged by examining the aims, content and pedagogy of individual subjects of the curriculum. Late nineteenth- and early twentieth-century accounts may be compared with those of the last 20 years. Philosophy for the last grade of the upper secondary school had much in common at least in approach in the two periods even though the topics changed. The comment of the early twentieth century was that it emphasized the examination, analysis and classification of ideas and their arrangement into a coherent whole – something that was felt to be lacking in equivalent schools in England.[15] A comparison might be made with the examination questions for philosophy in the *baccalauréat* in 1988. While some are contemporary – (How can the journalist decide that an event is historic? For what reasons should one respect nature?) – the majority are relatively timeless – (How can one hold to be true what has not been proved? Can taste be taught? Is it within the capacity of the State to limit its power? Can peace be made? Is there a virtue of forgetfulness? Is passion a mistake?)[16]

This intellectualism featured strongly also at earlier stages of secondary schooling. Moral education for 13-year-olds in the early twentieth century was treated historically and sociologically[17] and encouraged children 'to look at moral issues from an intellectual rather than an emotional viewpoint'.[18] The basic texts were the fables of La Fontaine but the exercises were firmly rationalist, including for instance questions such as: 'Distinguish modesty from humility.'[19]

Though applying to an older age group (15–18), the aims of the upper secondary curriculum of 1985 differ little:

1. *to give to the student the mastery of the junction between the abstract and the concrete*
Upper secondary students should know how to *conceptualize*, that is to say to move from confused global representation to clear ideas, to *analyse* which is to order their thinking, to *model* which is to construct abstract models which serve to understand reality and to act upon it. They should understand that the comprehension of the concrete is arrived at necessarily through theory and that the aim of the abstract is to allow precise understanding of the concrete.[20]

Yet some subjects, such as mathematics, are by their nature abstract and logical while others, essentially, have other goals. How can there be any rationalist mathematics when all mathematics would appear to be logical in whatever culture it is situated? How can there be a rationalist language study which has primordial goals of communication, expression and access to a literature which represents a (national) culture? How can history be rationalist when there can be 'only one safe rule for the historian: that he should recognize in the development of human destinies the play of the contingent and the unforeseen'?[21]

These subjects are forced into a rationalist mode in the encyclopaedic tradition of the curriculum. French mathematics teaching in secondary schools in the early twentieth century emphasized the exact presentation of theorems by students (often in front of a class ready to pounce on logical omissions) and on a rapid coverage to provide a grasp of the structure and unity of the whole subject at the expense of the endless working of examples which characterized English mathematics teaching.[22] In the 1960s, French mathematics teaching still insisted on the communication of rules and the incorporation of 'modern' mathematics within this framework.[23]

The logic of language, whether mother tongue or foreign (ancient or modern), would seem to be contained in its linguistic structures. This is the broader justification for language teaching (and the entry point for minority languages such as Breton or Arabic in the French curriculum in the 1970s). But rationality can be about doing as well as knowing and actual language teaching (mother tongue or foreign) concentrates on improving the capacity of students to structure and polish their French expression. Latin and Greek teaching in France in the early twentieth century gave far less attention than in English schools to translating into the classical languages and more to producing the most perfect translation into French.[24] In French the emphasis was not on learning rules of grammar but on developing skill with expression in the language – oral and written. Most particularly there was the search for overall structure, exactitude and balance.

> The French writer is not a mere framer of happy phrases [as in England]. His chief glory consists in his skill in building up phrases into paragraphs and paragraphs into one single harmonious, symmetrical, architectural whole.[25]

In history, the search was for perception of overall unity and structure in the subject. There was rapid and, for English eyes, superficial coverage, but a search for meaning in the chronological patterns and attempts to find unity in the diversity of political, cultural, social, economic movements in any one period.[26]

Rationality is not simply logic. It involves total comprehension through the construction of models and systems. Synthesis is important as well as analysis. It involves precision and exactitude in expression and communication. All through, the whole is more important than the parts and appreciation of structures is more important than any loss of depth.

The Enlightenment view of social, economic and political development, which was incorporated in the aims of revolutionary governments after 1789, was that rationality was the means to reconstruct society and its institutions in the most efficient, progressive and beneficial way. The means to development was central direction by a rationally trained élite. In this sense, encyclopaedism, through its emphasis on rationality, was directed at social usefulness, though the rational élite consisted of generalists rather than technical specialists.[27]

Later twentieth-century interpretations of utility have focused on more specific technical skills. The vocational sector of upper secondary education expanded from apprenticeship centres to a wider range and higher level of vocational courses in *lycées professionels*, which offered some courses of equal status to general academic upper secondary schooling including entry to higher education, especially technological higher education.

Technician level courses were then articulated, from the late 1960s, with general education not only in standing but also in content. That is, *baccalauréat* courses in specific branches of engineering, for instance, were based on a content (of both scientific and other general education subjects) which was common to the general *baccalauréat*. This process derived from élite education where the most prestigious higher education institutions since the early nineteenth century – the *grandes écoles* – were professional schools offering broad general education but, in most cases, giving a final qualification in engineering.

However, there is sequential progression in the three principles of universality, rationality and utility. Rationality can be developed once the framework for the transmission of a universalist curriculum is established. Utility becomes relevant once rationality has been developed. The difficulty of calling up the utility principles to justify courses at upper secondary level is that, by common understanding, rational education has hardly been completed – indeed, little more than begun – at that stage, so utility cannot be built clearly on rationality. The response of French students, their parents and employers has been to deny credibility to lower-level vocational education and to aim for higher-education-level vocational qualifications.

Debates about encyclopaedism in France

The French are encyclopaedist because they believe this is the route to liberty, equality and fraternity. Durkheim's major history of French education was a heroic story of the struggle of the forces of encyclopaedic progressiveness against humanist reaction.[28] Pierre Bourdieu's 'cultural capital' is humanism – acquired informally by the *mondain* who demonstrates it in 'effortless elegance'. For him encyclopaedism (or scholasticism) is egalitarian knowledge which is denied social equality by the operation of a humanist 'ethos of elective distance'.[29]

Encyclopaedism is not as rigid or exclusive as it was in the nineteenth and early twentieth centuries when it took on the character of an unremitting crusade against the forces of ignorance, superstition and reaction. A distinction has been made between nineteenth-century scientism and twentieth-century formalism.[30] Scientism emphasized the importance of learning all branches of knowledge and especially the non-literary sciences. It was associated intellectually with Auguste Comte's positivism and politically with the attack on the literary and classical humanism of the *Ancien Régime*. Its view of knowledge creation was inductive. Its structures were empirically created.[31]

Late twentieth-century encyclopaedism on the other hand is formalist. It stresses rationality to be achieved by deduction, analysis and the creation of parsimonious structures. It is 'what remains when everything else has been forgotten'.[32] In more elaborated form 'reason should not be used as a means of acquiring knowledge, but knowledge should be a mean of perfecting reason'.[33]

This abstract approach to thinking and analysis is not new. It dates back to medieval scholasticism. The criticisms made of it were those notoriously associated with angels on pinhead methodologies. As Pierre Emmanuel argued,

> We baptize as 'method' a clever trick that functions no matter to what object one applies it ... Thus intelligence by habit has come to be identified with this trick, with this infallible procedure for emptying an idea of all substance and the real of all reality.[34]

Since the 1960s there have been calls to introduce interrogative, communicative and social elements into logical analysis. Interrogative culture involves asking questions of oneself to establish 'what one does not know' (in line with the trends in Anglo-Saxon educational culture associated with the ideas of Karl Popper) and to situate thought in a social reality.[35]

However, these criticisms (which have been made across epistemological cultures since the 1960s) are made within the encyclopaedic tradition. Rationality had its limits but ultimately civilization as known in encyclopaedic cultures is rationalist. The alternative is not its destruction but its enrichment.

These debates have also applied in educational and pedagogical discussions in encyclopaedist cultures not only at a philosophical level but also through the dilemmas and difficulties of applying an encyclopaedism derived from élite nineteenth-century education to diverse and democratized mass education systems. These questions are explored in Chapter Three.

The encyclopaedic curriculum in southern Europe

How strong is encyclopaedism in the other countries of the European Community? In the projected future battle over a pan-European school curriculum, what allies can France expect to get? At some levels, encyclopaedism is part of the educational traditions of every country of continental (but not insular) Europe from the Soviet Union to Portugal and from Norway to Italy – a product not only of the historic impact of the Enlightenment and of the 1789 French Revolution.

The encyclopaedist south of Europe followed French institutional practice almost slavishly in the nineteenth century. Central control of the school curriculum until 30 years ago was almost identical, as have been the kinds of subjects and number of hours devoted to each subject in schools, the types of final school certificate, the processes of entry to higher education and the structure of courses in universities. Southern European countries have looked to France also for intellectual inspiration in the adoption of philosophies of worthwhile knowledge to underwrite the school curriculum. The forms and ideas of encyclopaedism are as much sacred idols in Italy, Belgium, Spain and Portugal as they are in France.

Like Spanish encyclopaedism, that of Italy is debased by its loss of the almost moral status that rationality has had in France. So encyclopaedism can degenerate into meaningless knowledge – into the 'rhetoric' or 'baggage' which Antonio Gramsci condemned.[36] It faces a more powerful naturalism in Italy than in France – a demand that schooling should reflect everyday concrete experience of children which is contained not only in the critical literature[37] but in the way that teachers behave and view themselves.[38] There is also the idealism – the search for a higher but as yet uncomprehended unity – reflected in the influence of Benedetto Croce in Italy but which has its parallels in the tradition of the yearning for the grand and sublime in Spain.

Despite these variations, the rational principles of encyclopaedism are defended by the critics of its sterility. So, for Gramsci the school:

> taught a more modern outlook based . . . on an awareness . . . that there exist objective, intractable natural laws to which man must adapt himself if he is to master them in turn – and that there exist social and state laws which are the product of human activity, which are established by men and can be altered by men in the interests of their collective development.[39]

His criticism of encyclopaedism is not about the emphasis on the abstract and formal learning of structures and connections. This is essential. What needs to be changed is only that students should carry on this learning actively and creatively rather than passively or without comprehension.[40] The progressive and liberating potential of encyclopaedism is affirmed even by its critics outside France.

Humanism

As a European intellectual movement, humanism 'meant the development of human virtue . . . not only such qualities as . . . understanding, benevolence, compassion, mercy – but also . . . fortitude, judgement, prudence, eloquence.' It had the aim of linking thought and action in ways that would encourage the grandest of human possibilities in the individual and would project the highest possibilities of the individual into the state at large.[41] Its source for Renaissance humanists from Petrarch onwards, was the classical literature of, for instance, Plato, Cicero or Livy. It focused on the individual rather than the social group. It was moral in its emphasis on the development of human virtue but this morality was extended to include aesthetic appreciation and sensibility. In a debased form, it was associated with etiquette and polite behaviour and so was linked even more to social differentiation.

The principles of educational humanism in England and Wales

The humanist perspective on education, as entrenched in the reformed public schools and ancient universities of mid-nineteenth-century England,[42] had three major principles:

- morality
- individualism
- specialism.

Nineteenth-century upper-class education set out to create 'Christian gentlemen'. The qualities to be needed by this élite were moral sensibility, a commitment to duty and a capacity for decision-making based on action informed and moderated by contemplation.[43] The explicit model was the philosopher-ruler class of Plato's *Republic*.[44]

The source of élite education was not only academic study. The social organization of the public schools and universities was intended to be educative – the *esprit de corps* of the games field, and the relations between students, and between students and teachers. Literary education focused on classical texts for the moral insights and examples they might yield. The epitome of this curriculum was the classics course at Oxford – two years of Latin and Greek language and literature, leading to the pinnacle of the final two years of Literae Humaniores ('Greats') of Greek and Latin history and philosophy.

In the twentieth century, the emphasis moved to British (English) history and literature. The purpose was still the development of moral capacities. English history, following the Whig interpretation, had the motif of the heroism, the duty, but especially the moderation of the historical actors who produced what was seen to be the finest democratic polity. Literature could focus on the works of the supreme English humanist – Shakespeare. Over time history and literature were democratized. The social history of the poor became more important while literature was chosen which reflected the condition of the poor and the ordinary people. Democratization meant simply making the élite aware of the lives and struggles of the poor rather than making humanist education available to a wider section of the population.

Other subjects struggled for recognition. Mathematics and the natural sciences had notional equality in the public schools and universities, though their informal prestige was lower, whether indicated by the lower status of science teachers at the public schools[45] or by the absence of science specialists in the political and managerial élite.[46] Science, it seemed, gave little insight into human virtue – except that, at one remove, scientific inquiry was claimed to be a highly moral activity. Mathematics at most developed aesthetic appreciation of mathematical rules. Bereft of the rationalist panoply which was so important to the encyclopaedist justification, mathematics, sciences and, indeed, modern languages (except as a means of access to morally enhancing fine literature) were not easily admitted to the inner sanctum of humanist high status knowledge.

Technical-vocational subjects were completely outside the humanist pale. In the Platonic social system, 'training' was associated with the occupations of social groups markedly inferior to the philosopher kings for whom a humanist education was designed.[47] The 'education v. training' dichotomy became particularly acute in societies where the humanist tradition was pre-eminent. Training was rejected in English education because of its contemporary social-occupational associations but also because it appeared to contain no possibilities for the development of moral sensibility.

The moral criterion remained central as humanist perspectives infiltrated the state education system. The process of transfer was aided partly by a belief that democratization of the curriculum meant dissemination of élite knowledge to a mass school population. It was facilitated also by the predominantly moral orientation of late-nineteenth-century mass education produced by the origin of many state schools in the religious system and by the largely moral socialization function of mass schooling which, in nineteenth-century England, unlike almost all other European countries, was established in an overwhelmingly industrial and urban society.

Individualism is central in the humanist world. Virtuous individuals create a moral world. Yet individualism is also central to the humanist conception of how humanist knowledge and humanist moral attributes are acquired. Humanism entails an individualist methodology and pedagogy.

The humanist methodology of learning, following Plato, is intuitive.[48] The learner thus reacts individually even idiosyncratically, to the set texts which are the containers of potential moral enlightenment. Standardized, methodical, systematic learning are not reconcilable with this intuitive view of education. Even élite traditional academic knowledge was acquired at the learner's own pace, indeed, to use a religious analogy, until revelation occurred.

Pedagogy was also individualist. The moral purpose of education gave a great stress to the interaction between teacher and student. Teachers, traditionally in English education, had a pastoral as well as an intellectual function. They had to know their pupils sufficiently well to direct them individually towards total moral development. The tutorial system of Oxford and Cambridge was a model for the rest of the élite education system.

The individualism of the humanist tradition permitted connections with more naturalist, child-centred philosophies. Indeed, John Locke, whose prescriptions on the moral education of the gentleman were a major source for the revived humanist education of the nineteenth century, advocated active and child-centred approaches in the early years of schooling.[49] Individualist and humanist views co-existed and were confused in the comprehensive schools in the 1960s and 1970s.

The degree of specialization in the curriculum of schools and institutions of higher education throughout the twentieth century has separated England and Wales from all other countries of Europe (including Scotland) – and, indeed, from every other country world-wide except those directly influenced by British colonialism. The English version of the humanist curriculum is marked by an early and intense concentration on a limited range of specific subjects and even on particular topics within subjects.

Subject specialism is permitted rather than required by humanist philosophy. Yet specialization can be reconciled with humanism. The attainment of moral sensibility does not depend in any way on width of knowledge but on depth of perception and understanding. The addition of other subjects may weaken the intensity of moral enlightenment achieved by student interaction with specialist topics.

Subject specialism is also encouraged by individualism. If learning is specific to the individual then a selection of appropriate knowledge – from the range of acceptable sources – can be made in relation to individual needs. Hence the maxim that students should be able to concentrate on the subjects for which they have a special aptitude to the neglect of those in which they have little interest or ability.

One puzzle is that English specialism is not paralleled in the humanist traditions in other countries. Two other features of English epistemo-logical culture then become important. First is the empirical approach to scientific inquiry which had its British roots in the epistemology of Francis Bacon and David Hume but which began to find expression in the development of research in universities in the nineteenth century. It was indicated in the expansion of single subject Honours schools at Oxford and Cambridge in the nineteenth century as the basic form of undergraduate study, which spread later to the other and newer universities. The inductive, empirical rationale for specialism is that knowledge is created cumulatively and incrementally out of small-scale inquiries from which eventually (often in hope rather than reasonable expectation) broad conclusions and patterns might emerge.

Empiricism and induction of this type could be supported in the absence of a rational tradition of logical analysis and theoretical system-building. The English version of humanism could be anti-rational. Intuition was more important than reason and intuition could be given scope in depth studies rather than in broad, schematic intellectual architecture. This empiricism also enriched the self-view of the English as having a bent for practical action.

Debates about humanism in England

The humanist tradition may have survived the democratization of education in England from the mid-twentieth century, but it has changed in the process and has been subject to criticism from the 1960s. The attacks have been made on two grounds – that the humanist view of knowledge is associated with a contempt for the material world of industry and trade and that socially it is ineluctably élitist. Perhaps most seriously, humanism is anti-rational in a world which is increasingly built on rational procedures.

The putative association of the humanist view with social élitism should be examined carefully in light of the attempts to democratize the humanist curriculum in the twentieth century. Moral appreciation of the great feats of ancient Greece and Rome – and later of English history – archetypically would encourage a muscular heroism in a District Officer in an African colony. In the course of the twentieth century, the occupational model became the sensitive aesthete – the television producer, teacher of English or advertising agency executive.

This change was linked to the emergence of English Literature as the most prestigious area of study in universities and upper secondary schooling. English Literature as defined by F.R. Leavis, the guru of the new sensibility, was supreme because

> it trains, in a way no other discipline can, intelligence and sensibility together, cultivating a sensitiveness and precision of response and a delicate integrity of intelligence[50]

This view was anticipated by earlier literary critics from the early nineteenth century, including Samuel Coleridge, Matthew Arnold and T.S.Eliot.[51] In the twentieth century it meant a different kind of élite selection. The assumption is that delicate intelligence is not necessarily the preserve of a traditional upper class. It is still assumed to be thinly distributed in the population as a whole. The discovery of submerged artists and aesthetes became the crusade particularly of teachers of English in secondary schools from the 1950s.

This new humanism was even more susceptible to charges that it was disdainful of the world of industry and hostile to vocational education. Politicians complained that schools encouraged anti-industrial attitudes among students which were associated with the declining productivity and international competitiveness of British industry. An increasing number of studies of the persisting aristocratic values of British society and anti-industrial attitudes were influential.[52]

The reaction of government was to attempt to initiate curriculum change which challenged a view of worthwhile knowledge which appeared to aim at nurturing an artist 'refined out of existence, indifferent, paring his fingernails'.[53] The national curriculum of the 1988 Education Reform Act tries to ensure that all students up to the age of 16 continue to study mathematics, sciences and technology which would otherwise be neglected in the preparation of aesthetes.

Do the changes culminating in the 1988 Act really challenge the social élitism and the anti-rationalism of the humanist tradition? The propositions of the 1943 Norwood Report that three types of children

– the academic, the technical and the practical – can be identified at the age of 11[54] have been rejected ostensibly with the spread of comprehensive schooling in the 1970s. It is not clear that such views, which harmonize with a humanist conception of knowledge, have been eradicated from the collective educational and national psyche.

Humanism outside England

Humanism is a European-wide – indeed global – movement since Islamic, Hindu and, especially, Confucian thought contains points of contact, particularly in a shared conception of the moral purpose of knowledge.[55] Historically, humanism is among the most powerful intellectual forces in Europe and may yet be revitalized by connections with these non-European parallels.

Educational humanism has points of similarity on an international scale. The emphasis on the development of the individual rather than on understanding the world; the concern for the attainment of individual human goodness through education; a belief that understanding comes first through intuition; and a prime focus on the study of the humanities (literature, history, philosophy) are common to educational humanism throughout Europe and beyond.[56] Indeed there is also a North American educational humanism associated with élite institutions of higher education.[57]

English humanism is other- rather than inner-directed. The educational humanism of the nineteenth-century public school was designed to produce men (very rarely women) of action. Thought was to inform the deed in a positive, energetic way. Moral sensibility was of value ultimately only in practice. Philosophers were to be kings and not simply philosophers (as were, for instance, the Brahmins of the Hindu system). The individual was educated through acquaintance with historical heroism, but in order to find his or her own way to be heroic in the present and future.

European humanism generally has been more inner-directed, contemplative, socially passive and politically quietist. It has concentrated upon inner contemplation and perfection divorced from action. Humanistic education has eschewed the search for social improvement. Thus it has been associated with a passive acceptance of existing patterns of social authority, especially the European Catholic version. But not only Catholic: a Greek Orthodox version of humanism is entrenched in education in Greece and is the enemy of political and social change (see below pp. 106–9). In these instances, humanism is socially and politically retrograde.

Humanist conservatism has been identified by both pragmatists and encyclopaedists as the main enemy of progress. John Dewey's attack on Platonic epistemology was central to his educational writing.[58] The rejection of humanism by Durkheim and Bourdieu in France has already been described. In return humanists have reinforced their conservatism by their total rejection of pragmatism – not only Europeans such as Jacques Maritain but also Americans such as Robert Hutchins.

Inner-directed humanism, however, takes on a quite different perspective in the German metaphysical tradition. The purpose of German education is humanist in that it is 'ethical and . . . is concerned primarily with the moral personality and with the inner freedom of the individual'.[59] But this humanist individualism aims to achieve individual understanding of the 'inner reality and unity in the cosmos'.[60]

The outcome is a greater individual moral awareness – even the quest for this understanding is morally enhancing. The means to the acquisition of knowledge is revelatory, intuitive, spiritual and mystical as well as rational. The subject matter for this search for total understanding can be the humanist works of literature and history. Yet this search for *Bildung* is inner-directed or other-worldly. Indeed, German élite education has been separated from public life and a public purpose to a degree that is totally foreign to the French or the English traditions.[61]

Furthermore German *Bildung* incorporates but stretches beyond a simple appreciation of humanity. It unites humanity and the world. It searches for rational understanding of the order of the natural world as well as an intuitive appreciation of human morality. It incorporates encyclopaedic rationalism as well as humanist moralism. So humanism does not exist by itself in opposition to rationalism but as part of a unity of all kinds of thinking and knowledge.[62]

In practice, these great ideals remain the holy grail of ambition rather than a reasonably attainable goal – especially in the secondary education system. German philosophy from Kant and Hegel to Habermas has sought means to achieve this transcendental unity. The search is real enough to inform the way that knowledge has been transmitted in élite education. But the proof of attainment is undemonstrable.

This leads to the major weakness of humanism as a possible solution to the search for internationally common school knowledge. The individualism and morality associated with humanism have potential value in mass education in urban, industrial education which the rationalist encyclopaedist tradition has failed to offer effectively. But humanism is really only a powerful force in English education. It has this position because it has developed links with action and public morality which are missing from the relatively sterile humanist traditions of other parts of Europe. But the social élitism, the specialism and the failure to provide a meaning for rational or manual/physical expertise in English humanism ultimately deprive it of a wider international potential.

Naturalist views

The dominant views in the public education systems of Western Europe emphasize universal ideas at such a level of abstraction that they are valid irrespective of time or place. The preceding analysis has focused on the differences between humanism and encyclopaedism. Yet they share much which also separates them from the many other views of knowledge in which immediate uses rather than universal principles and the learner rather than the subject matter take precedence.

Naturalist views have a long history and considerable variety in Europe and beyond. Yet they have never been dominant because they have never captured the citadels of legitimate knowledge in élite education. But they have had sufficient impact on lower-level and non-élite education in various European countries for them to be considered seriously in identifying a possible European curriculum of the future, especially those elements which meet 'private' knowledge aspirations.

Naturalist views of knowledge take as a starting point concepts of how individuals develop in the 'real' world. These perceptions are then applied to programmes of formal education. They include concepts of the intellectual and moral development of children; of individualism and creativity; of interaction in social groups; and of vocational commitment.

They may start from broad views of the individual and his or her interaction with the natural world (Jean-Jacques Rousseau); they may give more emphasis to the local community (N.F.S.Grundtvig) or to work (Georg Kerschensteiner); they may focus more specifically on the nature of learning rather than on knowledge (Johann Herbart, Celestin Freinet, Maria Montessori); they may attempt to achieve a unity of psychology, sociology and pedagogy (Johann Pestalozzi, Friedrich Froebel, Ovide Decroly); or they may be designed for young children by philosophers committed to universal knowledge in the education of youth (John Locke, Immanuel Kant). They derive intellectually from psychology and sociology as well as from philosophy. Their authors developed their ideas in a wide range of European countries – those cited above came from France, Germany, Denmark, Switzerland, Italy, Belgium and Britain.

In this study, the main question is what place these naturalist views have in formal and informal education in various European countries. There are three main locations – the education of very young children as an extension of the ideal educative family; the tight-knit social grouping beyond the family; and the workplace. Their influence comes through the extension of the family upwards, the workplace downwards and the social group sideways into the school system and, with these incursions, the acceptance of epistemologies appropriate to the institutions of origin.

Naturalist views have had an influence in every European country. But they may be examined more fully in the specific cases where they were especially entrenched 'child-centred' education in England, 'work-orientation' in Germany, and community education in Denmark.

Child-centred epistemologies in England and elsewhere

Official support in England for a child-centred primary curriculum did not appear until the beginning of the twentieth century. The 1931 Hadow Report claimed that, in practice since the 1890s and especially since 1918 there had been an actual change in primary school teaching so that it

> handles the curriculum, not only as consisting of lessons to be mastered, but as providing fields of new and interesting experience to be explored; to appeal less to passive obedience and more to the sympathy, social spirit and imagination of children, relies less on mass instruction and more on the encouragement of individual and group work, and treats the school, in short, not as the antithesis of life, but as its complement and commentary.[63]

The last clause is crucial. The suggestion of a relationship of school-learning to the actual life of children was new. Yet English child-centred education in primary schools, which reached its apotheosis of official support in the 1967 Plowden Report, remained principally a pedagogy emphasizing individual and active learning rather than a re-ordering of the purposes and aims of knowledge content as happened, for instance, with the adoption of a progressive pragmatic view in the USA. A major criticism at the time of the Plowden Report was that schooling was to be aligned to child psychology rather than to children as individuals or to their social environment.[64]

This emphasis on pedagogy rather than content; on process rather than final goals; on the medium rather than the message continued to be supreme, especially as child-centred approaches moved into lower secondary education. Particular comprehensive schools began to develop a reputation for organizing the whole curriculum on the basis of individual learning and creative expression at the expense of a standardized timetable.[65] The debate then centred on how the active and individualist curriculum which had been well established in so many primary schools could be transferred wholesale to comprehensive lower secondary schools.

The extent of the pupil-centred pedagogic revolution in English secondary schools from the 1960s should not be exaggerated. As was argued previously, the humanist tradition has an individualist orientation and permits specialization. Prevailing intellectual currents in higher education, scholarship and research are inductive and empirical. 'Discovery methods' in lower secondary schools could derive as much from these characteristics of traditional élite knowledge as from the child-centred approaches of the primary school. In practice, the individualist curriculum of secondary schools did not usually mean the abandonment of school subject boundaries or rationales. Instead there was a development of choice and variety at school and even pupil level in the specialization in particular subjects – a rejection of standardization between schools and even between students within a school rather than a repudiation of the ultimate external and universal value of traditional subjects.

Child-centred views are less well-established in state school curricula of other European countries as a whole, though the difference is not as great as some English educationists habitually have claimed. The movement in the eighteenth and nineteenth centuries to view children as having special, individual patterns of development and needs for creative, autonomous expression was no less powerful in Germany, France, Italy and other countries than it was in England and it continues to have support among significant numbers of teachers, other educationists and parents. But the encyclopaedist insistence on the standardization of content of learning and the demand that all children should reach minimum standards of achievement restrained the total adoption of child-centred views of knowledge.

Instead an overt distinction between content and method became more important than in England where the division was blurred and content could be manipulated to suit the method or even united to form a coherence with method.

A child-centred pedagogy, in a limited interpretation that did not interfere too severely with a standardized content, was adopted to varying degrees and with differing amounts of official support in continental European countries. In Germany it had most official backing. The first all-German Reich law of 1920 on primary education was full of phrases such as 'learning through the senses', 'closeness to life', 'wholeness' and 'spontaneity'.[66] These ideas on primary education were re-emphasized by the Federal Educational Council in 1970 with a stress upon individual initiative, co-operation and problem-solving.[67]

In France, Italy and the Iberian states the movement is weaker. Reference in France is most frequently made to the approaches of, say, Freinet, who was concerned largely with method. Individual teachers may have subscribed to and pursued these methods which encourage collective activity (especially producing class newspapers)[68]. There has also been support for this approach in Spain. Belgium has an influential child-centred movement. But these pupil-centred orientations have had little impact on the standardized primary school curriculum content.

There are doubts about whether child-centred approaches adopted in practice actually mean any alteration of the content and even the structure of knowledge to be transmitted. At most they imply methods which encourage individual self-expression and possibly a rearrangement or flexibility in the sequence of knowledge transmission. In this sense, these child-centred approaches do not necessarily comprise a distinct and different view of worthwhile knowledge. They may not be sufficient to meet future 'private' knowledge demands.

Work and community centred approaches in Germany and elsewhere
There is a separate strand of the naturalist view which emphasizes the validity of knowledge which is connected to everyday living and the effective performance of social and work roles. They differ from dominant humanist and encyclopaedic views in that educative experiences are not necessarily intellectual. The central and shared assumption of these views is that knowledge and attitudes can be acquired by means other than literary study and intellectual exercise.

Of course, accent on activity, on co-operation in collective tasks and on the tactile as well as cognitive is found in child-centred approaches generally. The main difference in the work and community orientation is that knowledge and attitudes gained have the aim of strengthening social bonds and affinities with actual communities and with real work-roles.

The community orientation has been the weaker of the two. The school as a medium for the discovery and strengthening of local community identity – and as a medium for the exploration and transmission of knowledge relevant to this aim – has been rarer in European traditions than in other continents such as Mahatma Gandhi's Basic School, or 'popular' schools in Latin-America. Examples such as the Folk High School in Denmark, inspired by Grundtvig, which tried to incorporate the activities of the community into education, were relatively rare. Indeed Grundtvig's Folk High School, like Paulo Freire's programmes in Latin America, were aimed primarily at adults.

Instead schools are organized more often as communities of children, which may have mirrored communities of the wider world – most frequently a concept of the traditional village community the admirable values of which child-centred advocates such as Pestalozzi, Froebel and, in the USA, Dewey sought to preserve in a collective and active pedagogy. But active learning, individual choice and freedom of expression and co-operative activities of students was based upon an nostalgic view of disappearing rural communities rather than the real worlds that children inhabited.

The major link between school knowledge and that of the wider community has been found in the pre-vocational curriculum as it emerged in a number of countries. The views of, say, Kerschensteiner in Germany on vocational education in the late nineteenth and early twentieth century did differ in a radical way from those of his mentors such as Froebel, in that Froebel, like other advocates of a child-centred view, took the psycho-physiological development of children as the starting point and wished to adapt the content of learning to this development. Kerschensteiner, in approaching the issues more crudely, did question epistemological foundations by arguing that knowledge of practical, vocational manual skills that students would later use as workers was as important as knowledge derived from books.[69] In this, his view, though crude like that of Gandhi, was also revolutionary in the way that Gandhi was revolutionary.

The assertion that the learning of manual 'trades' could be as valid in schools as knowledge derived from books was anathema to the Platonic view of high level education. As such it was rejected, for instance, in England. Yet in Germany especially, but also to a lesser extent in a Catholic technical school tradition in Italy and other parts of southern Europe, there was a view that knowledge about a manual vocation was noble and morally enhancing. The origin in part was religious – Christ the Carpenter and the Christian acceptance of humility and resignation to the earthly human lot. It crossed the Protestant-Catholic divide in Germany and was also founded upon a particular German cultural view that every occupation required training, every occupation had dignity and the work of every occupation should be carried out with maximum commitment and thoroughness.

The particular expression of this view in the Federal Republic of Germany is the *Arbeitslehre* which was introduced in the 1960s. This involved work experience as well as formal classes in schools. It was intended to encourage work habits such as self-discipline, consistency and social responsibility, as well as learning 'generic' cognitive and motor skills. It was epistemologically radical in the sense that the intellectualism and bookishness of the encyclopaedic and humanist traditions were put aside. Yet it simply brought the 'workplace' and the epistemology of work into the school and this epistemology of work – though perhaps more formally and institutionally expressed in Germany than in other European countries – was not uniquely German.

Naturalist views of knowledge mean, at one end, bringing the approaches of the early education of the child in the family into the school, so the reference points are the nature of growth in a child and the requirement of a pedagogy which takes account of all aspects of a child's development. Generally child-centred approaches represent a pedagogical rather than an epistemological challenge. There is little sense that these views do any more than prepare eventually for the closing of the prison house doors on the growing child and the introduction of real intellectual learning. And these approaches can be weakened by the counter-movement, with the growth of social welfare and 'compensatory' pre-school education, increasing intrusion of the formal school into the educative family.

At the other end naturalist views mean bringing work into school – that is, anticipating the epistemology and pedagogy especially of skilled trades and professions within schools. This was resisted very largely because the trades brought into schools were those conventionally associated with lower social/occupational levels and because of the aspirations that school should provide for a life wider than that of work and that it should also facilitate upward occupational mobility. But the major factor operating against this kind of vicarious transfer is the degree to which work itself is seen to require increasingly higher initial levels of school-transmitted knowledge attainments before students can be admitted into increasingly intellectualized real working occupations.

The third and marginalized element of the naturalist perspective is the view that school knowledge should inculcate private, and usually subordinated, community values. Yet school knowledge of this type does not attract support precisely because it fails to provide entry to 'public' and dominant institutions of later life (indeed private knowledge is little more than sharing of social closeness and thus the acceptance of a very limited range of small community mores). It has rarely had much impact in Europe – outside limited religious and linguistic communities – because alienation from public institutions has never been sufficient to force any orientation of major areas of schooling away from 'public' life.

The two dominant and public educational epistemologies – encyclopaedism and humanism – themselves have such obviously apparent weaknesses, that naturalist views of knowledge are very likely to be called in to shore up these flawed yet dominant epistemologies against their own contradictions – not least their foundation on traditional élite education.

Chapter Three
The Encyclopaedic Heartlands

A rationalist ideology prevails in southern Europe. Political ideals, administrative practice and educational philosophy converge into a coherent view of public knowledge and public action. Can rationalism accommodate the democratization of education, the conditions of urban industrial society and future private aspirations?

Some states are more central in this world than others. Italy, Spain, Portugal and Belgium mainly acquired an encyclopaedic conception of knowledge in the baggage of the conquering Napoleonic armies. They developed a less pure form of rationalist education as a result. They may have greater chances of developing alternatives to the intellectual bondage of encyclopaedism. In France, in contrast, educational debate has been vigorous yet it has been the application of encyclopaedism that has been its subject rather than the validity of the true faith.

France
Rationalism is part of historic European culture, yet it has been taken over by the French as their own and has permeated every aspect of public life in France. Reason has become central to those French mental attitudes which are treasured and habitually exhibited by individuals. Rationalism has penetrated educational culture to a degree which is unparalleled in the rest of Europe.

This ingrained rationality has given qualities to French education which are notably lacking in Britain. Yet the collectivist ethos of French education gives it a rigidity which, in common with Britain but in very different ways, is very badly aligned to a likely European future.

The context: political, economic and social change
State education in France takes its character from the collectivist

government which prevailed in the nineteenth and twentieth centuries. Each major institution of French education – except the university – had its origins in attempts to extend the power of central government. Rational encyclopaedism is the epistemology of the collectivist state *par excellence*. So the context of encyclopaedic education is the political system. In contrast, economic and social changes have been potential threats to the integrity of this view of education.

Collectivism is associated with the Jacobin assumption of power in 1792 – though it had antecedents in the monarchy of Louis XIV from the middle of the seventeenth century. Centralism has survived despite the accession of elected parliamentary government from 1871. It was only from the 1970s that limited devolution began. Yet even in the 1980s most decisions of public policy – from economic development to internal security and including social services such as education – were taken in Ministries in Paris and were transmitted through a hierarchical structure of administration at regional and local level.

The Jacobin world view was that social modernization was initiated by a corps of rational administrators who controlled centralized state institutions. From 1792, the imperative was to secure the gains of the 1789 Revolution, which meant the destruction of the power of the monarchy, aristocracy and church thus guaranteeing the position of a free, land-owning peasantry. It was dictatorial and anticipated the military rule of Napoleon I. French elite secondary schools – the *lycées* – and the prestigious *grandes écoles* at higher education level were products of Jacobin-Napoleonic collectivism. They functioned to produce rational public leadership through a 'career open to talents'. Inevitably the *lycées* were centrally controlled and had a standardized curriculum.

Collectivism of a different kind brought universal state primary education. The Third Republic, established following defeat by Prussia in 1871, was threatened by forces on the 'right' – especially monarchists who derived support from the landowners and church in the countryside. The expansion of state elementary education through the laws of Jules Ferry from 1879 to 1889 was designed to place a civilian army of school-teachers in the provinces to ensure the loyalty of the rural masses to the government in Paris.[1] In this context, state elementary education became anti-clerical and republican. Above all it became standardized and centralized.[2] These were the perfect conditions for the seed of an encyclopaedic curriculum to develop.

Advanced and often Utopian politics in France from the eighteenth to the twentieth centuries were acted out in its fevered brain in Paris rather than in the slow and lumbering body of a mass of peasants whose clocks, comfortably, stopped in 1789 when they gained their lands. Centralization usually meant attempts to bring in this body of peasants – often unaware of national politics and frequently unable to speak a language which was recognizably French – into harmony with political ideas in Paris. From the late nineteenth century it succeeded remarkably.[3]

There was little dynamic or creative challenge to Parisian dominance from provincial France. As a result, only élite education, designed to produce a national leadership, really mattered. Elementary schools aimed to turn peasants with local affiliations into patriotic French men and women. Apart from the small number of local *petits fonctionnaires* who gained their places on the basis of performance in the elementary school, universal schooling was not to disturb the centuries-old condition where the sons and daughters of peasants became peasants like their parents.

Industrialization provided the dynamic and creative challenge to centralized and encyclopaedic education. It was a long time coming. France had major industries in the mid-nineteenth centuries but it was not until after 1945 that the sea of agricultural France was claimed by the islands of industry. It was not until the 1960s that France became an urban society with urban values and a brand new high technology which put her among the industrial leaders of the world. Its impact on the settled condition of French education could have been devastating.

Yet rational education has partly conquered the seething diversity of industrialization. Centralized government has attempted to control and direct economic development through economic planning. Educational provision at secondary as well as higher level since 1950, and especially since the 1960s, has been dictated by the economic goals of *le plan*.[4] Rational encyclopaedism has been orientated towards a high-technology economy.

Industrial economy has been partly tamed. Industrial society has seemed more uncontrollable. First, there is the individualism of taste and aspiration which standardization cannot easily accommodate. There is diversity of cultures which is only partly accounted for by immigration from North Africa and Portugal in the 1960s. Most of all there is the need for socialization in urban settings where traditional family bonds have weakened. It is in these areas that encyclopaedic French education has encountered the greatest difficulty.

Changing school and changing curriculum

Until the early 1960s there were two systems of state schooling. Elementary education from 1882 was free, universal and compulsory up to the age of 13, but it was also terminal. A minority continued education in upper grade schools or in primary school teacher-education. Only in 1959 did secondary education begin to become available to all but only up to the age of 15 in *collèges d'enseignement général* which were roughly equivalent to English secondary modern schools or German *Hauptschulen.*

The *lycées* had recruited their students at age 11 from their own fee-paying preparatory classes. Only after 1945 were most of their students selected from state elementary schools. The *lycées* were often for a social as well as an intellectual élite. They could concentrate on the business of preparing a national leadership, especially since they were not faced with the competition of a prestigious independent school sector as in Britain.

This vertical division was replaced by a horizontal arrangement when the 1963 Fouchet Decrees introduced neighbourhood comprehensive lower secondary schools – the *collèges d'enseignement secondaire*, later simply *collèges*. The *lycées* were transformed into academic upper secondary schools. Curriculum upheaval followed this educational revolution. Other changes also contributed. Pre-school education expanded more quickly in France than in any other western European country apart from Belgium, so that 84 per cent of 4-year-olds were in school in 1970. A technical-vocational branch of upper secondary education grew rapidly. Enrolments in higher education exploded in the 1960s and had reached over 20 per cent of the age group by the early 1970s.

The expansion and democratization of education raised the question of whether the same knowledge menus should and could be offered for mass consumption as had been made available earlier to an élite. At school level, the answer was broadly in the affirmative. The results are impressive but at the cost of a narrowing of options for a more heterogeneous school population.

Primary schooling

Of all the sectors of French education, primary schools have been least affected by structural change. Compulsory schooling begins at six though almost all children have had three years of pre-school experience. Primary schools take their pupils through five grades. All children then transfer to local *collèges* without any formal selection. Conditions would seem favourable for the development of child-centred institutions.

French primary schools had been the agencies of a centralized nation state since the 1880s. Curriculum aims in 1985 emphasized that even primary school children should be taught the rights and duties of being French and their place in the national socio-political system. Rousseau's question of whether education should prepare a man (*sic*) or a citizen was answered much the same in 1985 as it had been after Jules Ferry's reforms from 1879.

Primary schools have not always been entirely alien bodies representing the wishes of a distant central government. Ferry's republican army of school teachers was not able totally to impose a central writ upon a sullen provincial population. They had to react to local circumstances to win acceptance by local communities.[5] Informal attempts to relate the experience of school to its environment developed in the spaces when the serious business of reading, writing, computation and French national history, geography and civics was temporarily left aside. Indeed, in the 1970s, the official curriculum suggested that history, geography, art, craft, science, moral education and music could be covered in an interdisciplinary or integrated way under the general rubric of 'curiosity awakening activities'.[6]

The individualist or community orientation in French primary schooling has always been fragile. The main purpose, as the 1985 curriculum bluntly stated, is teaching and learning.[7] The unassailable core has been language and mathematics. Achievement in these areas is crucial. Children are tested regularly by teachers, admittedly without heavy intervention from higher authority and often in close contact with parents. Failure means grade repeating which affected between 10 and 15 per cent of both first and final grade primary school pupils in the mid-1980s.

The achievement orientation prevailed in French primary schools even during the socially relaxed 1970s. In the hard-nosed mid-1980s, the primary school curriculum was directed even more to national rather than local or individual concerns. The 1985 regulations broke up the integrated *activités d'éveil* and returned to separate subjects with their own time allocations as well as introducing the new area of science and technology.[8] The national curriculum of prescribed subjects, time allocations, topics and objectives has been as strong in the 1980s as it was in the nineteenth century.

Changes have occurred to some extent in teaching methods and materials as well as in teacher openness to consultation. The traditional *explication de texte* where the teacher expounds in relation to a text, picture or object and then questions the class as a whole has not disappeared. But teachers have a greater choice of books and of other materials (indeed, unlike West Germany or even the USA, there is no exclusive list of books). They consult with each other about pupils and, more crucially, with parents in regular meetings. Indeed, they have considerable opportunity to introduce individual and group projects, though this is very unevenly accepted.[9]

There is almost a conspiracy among teachers and parents to pursue the national curriculum. They justify it by reference to the true equality of opportunity which a national curriculum and, informally perceived, national standards bring. Indeed, even pre-primary school teachers, encouraged by national directives, put much stress on encouraging the development of 'cognitive faculties'[10] especially to reduce primary school grade repeating and the trajectory of failure that this launches children upon.

Yet the primary school curriculum is only encyclopaedic by the limited criterion of universality (all subjects with a standardized content provided equally for all children). Primary schools do not aim specifically to develop rationality. But the standardized cognitive orientation of primary schools makes much more possible the serious attempt to inculcate rational intelligence in secondary schools.

Lower secondary schools

The establishment of the *collèges* switched attention to a common curriculum to achieve equality of opportunity for all. In practice, the *collège* curriculum has been modelled on what was previously offered in the selective long-cycle *lycée*. The main problem has been to make this curriculum digestible by the entire youth population.

At the beginning, pupils and teaching were differentiated according to expectations of achievement and future occupational role. The first two grades were termed the *observation* cycle followed by two grades of *orientation* – that is, differentiation which the *observation* cycle had guided. In practice, this meant streaming. The first two *filières* followed a broadly common curriculum, except that the fast stream could take options such as classical or additional foreign languages. The lowest of the three streams, the *classes de transition* and, in the third and fourth grades, the pre-vocational classes, were restricted to a diet of little more than French, mathematics, civics and craft.

A common curriculum was one aim of the 1975 Haby Law. A system of setting by achievement in individual subjects was proposed to replace streaming. A completely mixed ability first grade of the *collège* and the abolition of the *classes de transition* was proposed by the Legrand Commission in 1982. The outcome was a core curriculum of French, mathematics, a modern language, history, geography, civics and economics, experimental science, artistic education, technical and handicraft education and physical education. Distinctions between pupil abilities and future expectations in practice were reflected in the pace and level of teaching in different sets and in the selection of options (in practice Latin, Greek or a second foreign language for faster students, extra teaching in the first foreign language for the average, and technology for the slowest).

A common core curriculum was largely achieved for 70–75 per cent of the school population. The losers were those who failed to get access to a common curriculum not only through streaming but through grade repetition, which meant that they never reached the grade appropriate to their age. In practice, many of this group ended in vocational classes in separate institutions after two grades of general secondary education. The proposals on mixed-ability teaching of 1975 and 1982 failed to abolish these 'sink' classes for 14–16-year-olds.[11]

The search for a common curriculum in comprehensive schools reinforced the central place of the encyclopaedic universality. The eight-subject core curriculum covered 24 hours of the 27-hour week in the *collège*. Opportunities for school level or individual student choice were limited. The Haby Law had proposed that the content of 10 per cent of teaching time should be left to the discretion of individual schools. In practice, this time was usually devoted to extra classes on core curriculum subjects.[12]

The objective of rational thinking is marked in the requirements of individual subjects. The first of the three general aims of the *collège* curriculum of 1985 is to develop logical thought among students.[13] Throughout the objectives of individual subjects, 'reasoning' and 'method' figure prominently in, for instance, French, mathematics and biology. System building is important in history (chronological development), geography (spatial relations), and even foreign languages (linguistic comparisons with French). Indeed, the emphasis on rationality in 1985 was greater than in previous curriculum instructions, reflecting not only Minister Jean-Pierre Chevènement's concern with the 'information age', but also the maturity of the common secondary curriculum which could move away from the limited goal of universality towards the highest good of reason.

Utility also had a place in the objectives of the 1985 national curriculum but in the sense of aiming to produce good citizens rather than future workers. Five themes were to be treated across subjects boundaries – security, health, consumerism, the environment and development in the Third World.[14] These themes are common to 'social adjustment' approaches to the curriculum, especially derived from American pragmatism. In France they were put firmly in their place in the encyclopaedic scheme of knowledge. Students were to acquire basic facts about central subjects of knowledge. Then they were to develop their capacity for rational thought. Then they were to apply this rationality to matters of contemporary concern to responsible citizens.

Upper secondary (including vocational) education

Common schooling ends after four grades of lower secondary education. Upper secondary education is differentiated. Around 35 per cent of the age group goes to academic *lycées* which feed directly into higher education. Around 40 per cent of 16–19-year-olds are in some form of vocational education which, in some varieties, has equivalence with the *lycée* but which overall is a less well regarded sector.

Selection is less sharp than in England or even in the Federal Republic of Germany. The examination taken at the end of lower secondary schooling – the *brevet des collèges* – is only used to judge borderline cases of allocation to one form of upper secondary education or another. Only in three subjects – French, mathematics and history-geography-civics-economics – are standard written papers set and that was an innovation in 1986. Instead the continuous process of *orientation* over the last two grades of the *collège* is used to allocate students.

The rationale for allocation is national need rather than student ability. The 5-year national plans have forecast the proportions of the future work force required for specific occupations and educational provision has been tailored to these demands. The impact has been to legitimize the orientation of all students towards future occupations from the age of 14.

The three-grade general academic course in the *lycée* leads to the state examination for the *baccalauréat* which gives entry to higher education. In the final two grades students are required to choose among five main branches – philosophy and letters (with several sub-branches according to the weight on ancient or modern languages); economics and social sciences; mathematics and physical sciences; mathematics and biological sciences; mathematics and technology. This is a considerable extension of the two main branches (letters, mathematics) which prevailed in the *lycée* before 1945.

Specialization in the general *lycée* has not been allowed to undermine the encyclopaedic principles of universality and rationality. A common core curriculum remains in the first grade as in the *collège* except that optional subjects allow some specialization. In the last two grades, students are placed in a specific branch but each section follows all the subjects of the common core (so, for instance, all students will study French, mathematics, a modern language, sciences and history-geography). The differences are in the number of hours, the level and the form of examination for, say, mathematics for the letters or the mathematics-physics section.[15] Specialization is separated firmly from exclusivity.

The development of rational thinking is identified as the first general objective of all *lycée* courses and, as has been seen, this aim was clearly and fully elaborated in the 1985 curriculum prescriptions (see above p. 20).[16] However the main indicator of the dominance of the rationality criterion is the relative status of the different specializations. Branch C (mathematics and physical science) has a far higher standing than the other specialisms, so much so that there is competition to enter this option and students choose to repeat a year to have a second attempt to enter Branch C, rather than accept another option.[17]

Mathematics and physical science are seen to be the best preparations for key occupations in a high-technology economy. But the progressive ordering of the three criteria of encyclopaedism – universality then rationality then utility – has been applied so rigidly that lower-level vocational education has suffered. The accepted route, for students, employers and the higher education institutions, is a high level of abstract mathematical and scientific study leading to high-level scientific, technological and management training and occupations. Lower level technical occupations without the preparation of abstract, rational studies are more frequently shunned.

In the light of national economic plans, much weight was given to upper secondary vocational education from the early 1960s. A range of state institutions providing vocational education, but catering mainly for apprentices on a part-time basis, were united into a *collège d'enseignement technique* in 1960 which was upgraded into a *lycée d'enseignement professionel* in 1975 (later the *lycée professionel*) to indicate parity of status with the general *lycée*. The aim of upgrading worked for the high-level courses, especially the *baccalauréat de technicien* (later *baccalauréat professionel*) of 1968, which was run on the same pattern as the general *baccalaureat* except that the specializations were in more specific vocational areas (originally three main sections but later expanded to eight). This course did have status because it could lead to technological higher education and had a core of general, rational and scientific study.[18]

The major issue in vocational education has been the craft qualification, the *Certificat d'Aptitude Professionel* (CAP) for which the largest proportion of *collège* leavers prepare.[19] This is a specific vocational qualification with 260 branches studied mainly part-time by young workers over three years. While some British commentators have been impressed by the thoroughness of both vocational preparation and the high level of general education,[20] French educationists have been concerned with the high failure rates in the examination and the low prestige of the qualification among French students.[21] Classic encyclo-paedism seems to encourage students to have aspirations to become high-level engineers but to spurn the craft-level occupations which are highly sought even among graduates of upper secondary education in the Germany Federal Republic.

Curriculum issues and debates

Broadly there has been agreement in France since the 1970s on the desirability of a common national curriculum for common schools. The main difficulties have been how to make this accessible to all children and how to reconcile this aim with the simultaneous demand for occupational differentiation. There are also questions about whether 'national' knowledge should focus upon universal rationality or national political and cultural solidarity and about the extent that universal reason can be negotiated with individual pupils.

More difficult questions are raised about the place of private cultures in French education. The traditional antipathy to particularism in French state education has not weakened yet has made it difficult to reconcile many children and parents to the value of French education. It will make it even more difficult for future migrant children and their parents to accept French education.

Common school, national curriculum and universal knowledge

The common curriculum for a common school has met with difficulties. The first concerns the low achievers and slow learners. The attacks on differentiation in the 1970s and 1980s have not been entirely successful. School-teachers and principals have resisted assimilation. Low achievers in practice still tend to be set lower sights. The standard curriculum has been modified sufficiently to make it a reasonable target at some level for the majority of children. But the position of the lowest achieving group of students is still intractable. As in West Germany, emphasis on minimum standards of common achievement has isolated a new underclass of low achievers who seem not capable of being reached by national criteria of attainment.

There are also debates about the nature and place of the universal rationality which underlies the encyclopaedic view of knowledge. There are views that it should be interrogative, applying logic to reality without preconceptions about the answers. In schooling, this has tended to mean taking cognizance of the culture of the pupils. So logical linguistic patterns, for instance, may not be those of standard French but of the language used by children and the purpose of rational analysis is to find patterns in this changing , heterogeneous popular culture. Traditionalists have attacked this process as a denial of true universal reason.[22]

Yet many of the difficulties of the common curriculum centre on the interpretation of universal knowledge. The French encyclopaedist curriculum has been widely attacked within France by parents and pupils because it is over-intellectual and over-demanding in the amount of pupil time spent in learning large amounts of information.[23] One of the inherent difficulties of a universalist curriculum is that there is no criterion of exclusion except, at least in France, the rational, systematic structure of the knowledge to be learned. But even applying this standard, the amount of knowledge can expand exponentially.

After the 1975 Haby Reform, the response was to cover as wide a ground as possible but to deal with this thematically so that the systematic outlines could be perceived. So history, geography and even French gave more emphasis to international cultures.[24] There was a reaction in the 1985 curriculum and a return to more specifically French knowledge. History was to stress continuity rather than world-wide themes. *Collège* students were expected to have read 15 works of literature (mainly French with occasional 'good' translations).[25] There was a partial return in lower secondary education to the ideal of the nineteenth-century elementary schools, that education was designed to produce patriotic Frenchmen and women rather than the world citizens to which the 1975 curriculum had been moving.

The concept of rationality has been a unifying force in the French national curriculum but it has been offered in purest form to the more able students who go on to take the mathematics and physics branch of the *baccalauréat*. The adoption of a libertarian and relative view of rationality by 'radicals' in the name of popular schooling for the majority of pupils has been met by a reassertion of the centrality of French national political culture by the 'right'.[26] But neither approach has been able to balance the central importance of encouraging rational thought in the school population as a whole with the need, so far very ineffectively met, to cater for private cultures.

Private cultures in French schooling

The difficulties in meeting private cultures in French state education also stem from the historical origins of the system. State education spread to challenge the power of the Catholic church. It has been imbued with an anti-clericalism which survives even in the late twentieth century. It has also been associated in the past with the eradication of local cultures, particularly of regions such as Brittany.[27] In France, state schooling has been alien from the family, which it has complemented in the countries of north Europe or has been a substitute for as in England.

With these historical legacies, it has been difficult for the French school to throw off its position as an exclusively national institution. The church-state issue is not dead, as was seen in the controversies of 1982, when the socialist government attempted to reduce government aid to church schools and met successful opposition from supporters of these schools.[28] For many radicals, it is central government which is the potential defender of republican and socialist ideals. Particularism is conventionally associated with conservatism and reaction.

There have been some concessions to local and sub-cultural interests since the late 1960s. Minority languages, whether of geographically concentrated historic communities such as the Bretons, Basques, Corsicans or the people of Occitan, or of more recent immigrants especially from Portugal or North Africa, have been permitted alternatives to established modern languages in secondary schools since the early 1970s. But these concessions have not extended to other areas of culture such as history, literature, music and art.

The crucial issue for many teachers has been the alienation of children in an urban and heterogeneous society from the uniform state school. A diverse society is now challenging the uniform school which previously controlled and standardized it. At one level, this alienation is expressed in youth culture rejection of school. But this also suggests a wider gulf between significant social groups and the national school. But even the limited proposal of the Legrand Commission of 1982 that teachers should be required to undertake three hours of pastoral activity with pupils each week to come to terms with some of these social conflicts has been resisted by teachers.[29]

From 1981 the socialist government has made some response to youth alienation by the proposition of school-level multi-discipline curriculum projects (*Projets d'actions éducatives*) which would also use more concrete and diversified teaching methods.[30] But these schemes were linked to the Education Priority Zones of social disadvantage and educational under-achievement which were to receive extra funding.[31] The same curious logic was accepted as has been the case in other countries, that pedagogic innovation and an individualized or community orientated curriculum are most appropriate for 'educational failures'.

The irony is that education in France, which was historically founded on providing *culture générale*,[32] no longer transmits any culture which has real meaning to many of its students. Minister de Chevènement in 1985 appealed to the idea of a unifying technical-scientific culture. But this has little place for many private and community aspirations. It is in this sense that France has an education system that produces barbarians – that is, students who, though often intelligent and often scientifically efficient, fail to find a place in any kind of authentic non-scientific culture.[33]

Conclusion

Encyclopaedism emerged in France as a revolutionary and reformist view of the nature and function of knowledge in transforming society in the interests of the majority of its members. An encyclopaedist curriculum has allowed for a degree of equality of treatment of students that is not matched in most other European countries where encyclopaedism was weaker. It may be claimed also that an encyclopaedic curriculum has been suited to the economic transformation of France since the 1960s. The French education system has produced high-quality engineers and technologists that other countries have envied. The intellectual and professional qualities of the French administrative élite are widely admired. Both characteristics may be associated with an encyclopaedic approach to the curriculum.

In this respect, French education may be the most appropriate to a future high-technology-information society. French knowledge most exactly conforms to the technical requirements of such societies as identified by futurologists such as Daniel Bell or Alain Touraine. France may offer the standard in these areas for the rest of Europe.

French education has been the least successful among the major countries of western Europe in accommodating individualist and subcultural aspirations for private and community knowledge. As in Britain an obsolete national political culture is still seen as central in educational socialization. Unlike Britain or indeed most other European countries there is no widely accepted alternative culture or cultures. It is for this reason that French education, unmodified, is in danger of producing a society of technocratic barbarians.

Italy

By virtue of its size, economic power and culture, Italy ought to be a
major educational force in Europe. It is not. Public education in Italy,
like that of France, is an alien institution imposed on a rich local culture
by a remote central government. In France, this central government is
efficient and dynamic, deriving a legitimacy from the tradition of the
1789 Revolution. Public education in Italy is a distant and disconnected
arm of discredited central government rather than an outgrowth of a
vibrant local culture.

The weakness of the Italian central state is commonly explained by
the circumstances of its birth. The Italian nation was created by the
Piedmontese conquest of the rest of the country between 1859 and 1870.
Piedmontese institutions – which were very similar to those of France
– were imposed on the whole of Italy. Yet the nation was diverse. There
was no universally understood oral language and certainly no national
identity.

These divisions were obscured by the Fascist government of 1922–43
but not overcome by it. A parliamentary republic since 1944 has not
produced stable or forceful governments even though each administration has been basically Christian Democrat. Regional differences and
antagonisms have been overlaid at a national political level by the
ideological-political schism of Catholics and Communists. Local
particularism co-exists with national politics based on grand and
universal ideologies.

Lack of strong government has inhibited coherent national educational reform. Yet public education has remained under central control
and has suffered from local hostility to the arbitrary and swollen state
bureaucracy. Perhaps more important is the continuing north-south
economic division. In the later twentieth century an industrial economy
has developed in the north which is as advanced as any in Europe.
Southern poverty has remained and has not been alleviated significantly by massive emigration to the industrial areas of the north or
outside the country. The consequences of this divide have been that a
centralized Ministry of Education has had to cater uniformly with the
educational needs and demands of an advanced industrial region and of
areas of rural poverty where illiteracy remains high, double-shift
schools have been common and the effective provision of even full
primary education is insecure.

Italian state education dates from the 1959 *légge Casati* of Piedmont
which was then applied to the whole of Italy. This established a
centralized system of educational administration implemented by

provincial officials. It declared that secondary and higher education primarily should train a modernizing, professional élite on the French model. The difference from France was that, while education was to be predominantly secular, (Catholic) religious teaching should have a place in schools.[34]

The processes whereby encyclopaedism came to dominate school knowledge are more complex. Élite schooling was provided in the late nineteenth century in an upper secondary *licèo* which had classical and mathematical branches. A humanistic curriculum prevailed, supported by the central position of the study of classical languages and literature and of the Italian Renaissance. But humanism was overtaken by an encyclopaedic approach:

> though the classical languages were meant and were said to give the 'humanistic' spirit to young people, they lacked much of what is really humanist in the way they were taught. It became more and more the rule that Latin and Greek were studied as a training of the mind, somewhat similar to the training given by the study of logic and mathematics. An interest in the rules and irregularities of phonetics, morphology and syntax took the place of interest in the language itself as it was used to express the lofty thought and imagination of the classical writers.[35]

This change was a reflection of the dominance of the academic lower secondary (*ginnàsio*) curriculum in which mathematics and the sciences were more prominent.

Italian views of worthwhile knowledge also include 'idealist' Hegelian strands which were developed under the influence of writers such as Croce but embodied in the education law of Gentile of 1923. Though this law was associated with the Fascist government, its holism represented an older Italian view. It attempted to unite humanist, rational-encyclopaedist and naturalist principles in the school curriculum with the goal of reaching total understanding.[36] The result, however, was overloading and a consequent emphasis on acquisition of large amounts of information. Yet this holistic view was to reappear with the curriculum of the comprehensive lower secondary schools of the late 1970s.

Changes in school and in curriculum since the 1960s
The 1948 Constitution declared that education should be compulsory for children aged 6–14. This led to the establishment of common lower secondary schools after 1962. Democratization and reform have been

less evident in the restrictive and divisive system of upper secondary education which survives despite many proposals for change.

Primary education

The five-grade primary school has become general since common middle schools were established. It has a national curriculum of subjects and topics within them prescribed by the national Ministry of Education though the first two grades are concerned largely with the three Rs. For the final three grades, the prescribed subjects provide a link with post-primary education – religion, Italian, moral and civic education, history, geography, science, arithmetic and geometry, drawing, singing, practical work and physical education.

Though this curriculum is orientated towards standardized achievement there is much opportunity for teacher initiative in practice. Teachers are required to assess children regularly and systematically, though bald marks have been replaced by broader assessment cards. Grade repeating, the traditional form of quality control, had been reduced to little more than 2 per cent of pupils by the late 1970s. Teachers have considerable latitude in teaching methods and choice of textbooks and materials. With the introduction of common lower secondary education, the primary school leaving examination no longer dominates the curriculum. In practice a 'family' atmosphere may often prevail and a concrete approach to learning.

Lack of resources for primary education, especially in the poorer regions, is a major difficulty. Primary school teachers, uniquely in western Europe, have been trained in upper secondary education level institutions rather than in higher education which may have depressed their social standing and their confidence in re-orientating the primary school curriculum.

The middle schools

The common middle school was established following a law of 1962 which, in effect, united into one comprehensive school the various forms of upper elementary schooling and lower secondary education (except for the academic *ginnàsio* which joined the upper secondary *licèo*). By the mid-1970s almost all children aged 11–14 were in these three grade schools.

The national curriculum drawn up in 1977 for middle schools was conventional by European standards – Italian, mathematics, history, geography, civics, a foreign language, science, religion, technical education, musical education, artistic education, and physical education.[37] The broad objectives differed little from those of France with an emphasis on the development of logical, scientific and practical aptitudes but also on understanding the totality of the social world in all its facets and helping individual students to make choices in life.[38]

The precise objectives for individual subjects suggest links between the development of rationality and the acquisition of a total understanding of the world through a very substantial content. Language teaching (especially Italian) is to develop linguistic skills for daily use and as a means for the student to understand his or her own personal world. It should also include knowledge of 'the forms, structures, genesis and historical development of verbal communication' including, for instance, a knowledge of Latin in order to understand Italian.[39] Mathematics and science should

> aim at developing logical abilities and abstract and deductive thinking, as well as a scientific habit of mind so that problems are dealt with in a constructive and dynamic relationship with reality.[40]

The guidelines contain much grand rhetoric. The basic building blocks in the construction of fairy palaces of total understanding are logic and schematic systems. This rationality is the concrete element of Italian epistemology.

It is, of course, unlikely that these grand aims and total coverage will be attempted by teachers. Logic and reason are more attainable goals. But they are likely to be accompanied by attempts to demand substantial factual learning. This is encouraged by the emphasis in the middle school on teacher testing of pupils and the barrier to upper secondary education presented by the middle school leaving certificate, even though only Italian and mathematics are tested by written examinations.[41]

Upper secondary education
There has been less thorough reform of upper secondary education where there is a distinction between the five-grade academic schools (*licèi*) and various kinds of vocational education.

The two kinds of *licèo* (classical and scientific) both follow a broad core curriculum – religion, Italian, Latin, foreign languages, history, philosophy, geography, biological sciences, chemistry, physics, mathematics, drawing and physical education. There is only a slight difference in the time spent on science and humanities between the classical and scientific *licèi*.[42] Studies in both institutions lead to the *maturità* diploma which gives access to any university faculty. This curriculum is more traditionally encyclopaedic than its equivalents in most other European countries. Specialization has not been adopted despite several government proposals from the mid-1970s onwards.[43]

This lack of reform can be attributed to the relatively marginal position of the *licèo*. More than twice as many students attend technical institutes. These provide vocational education to full upper secondary level, include substantial amounts of general education in their courses and lead to qualifications which give entry to university.[44] The marginalization of the *licèi* may be linked also to the opening of access to universities from the late 1960s, when many were able to enter without conventional qualifications. Government efforts since the mid-1970s have been to try to control university enrolments more effectively.

The capacity for change in Italy, especially to modify a dominant encyclopaedic practice and to introduce more individual and community knowledge, should not be underestimated. There is a tradition of *de facto* local community initiative whatever the regulations of central government. There are traditions of a child-centred and community-orientated schooling despite rigid central regulations. So, ironically, the well-known critique of alienating centrally controlled education in the School of Barbiana's *Letter to a Teacher* is an example of the kind of teacher-pupil projects which reoccur in Italian education on a local and haphazard scale.[45] But this local vitality is more likely to be directed at the stars of 'cultural revolution' than the sands of detailed and systematic challenge to nationally controlled curriculum practice.

Spain and Portugal

These countries have had state education systems modelled closely on France since the mid-nineteenth century. Both countries experienced dictatorships for long periods in the mid-twentieth century during which state education was stagnant in economies that were backward. The accession of elected parliamentary governments in the 1970s has produced social, economic and political change which have major implications for education. These cases may allow consideration of a number of questions about the role of encyclopaedic education in industrializing economies with (in the Spanish instance) pluralist societies where governments are prepared to enact fairly radical educational change.

Spain

The adoption of French administrative and educational institutions in the nineteenth century was made possible by the waning of the power of imperial Spain, the Napoleonic occupation and the nationalist reaction against it. Political modernization in the twentieth century was brought to a halt by the Civil War, 1936–9, and the subsequent dictatorship of General Franco until 1975. This regime emphasized not only order and patriotism but gave considerable power in social affairs to a conservative Catholic church. Governments of the parliamentary monarchy since 1975 have embraced political ideas of social equality of opportunity and popular participation in public institutions. This has included recognition of a degree of autonomy for historic nationalities.

State education effectively was established by the Moyano law of 1857. The Ministry of Education had administrative control, decided upon the employment of teachers and determined the curriculum. The provision of elementary schooling was the responsibility of local communities and of secondary education that of provinces. The system differed from that of France mainly in that the national inspectorate was weak and a substantial proportion of enrolments was in church schools. While liberal governments in the late nineteenth and early twentieth centuries (especially those of the Second Republic, 1931–6) attempted to widen provision, reduce church influence and increase local participation, education changed little between 1857 and 1970.

Changing school and changing curriculum

The Basic School
The major reform was the 1970 Education Act. Indeed, it was a spectacularly radical measure by contemporary European standards. Eight-grade common 'basic' schools were introduced for children aged 6–14. The curriculum was teacher orientated and allowed considerable school-level decision. In the primary cycle there were five 'areas' – language expression, plastic expression, dynamic expression, mathematics, and society and nature. In the lower secondary stage, more conventional subjects were prescribed. The guidelines of content were only advisory and tentative. Teachers were to have considerable latitude in determining the precise content which they were encouraged to relate to the 'concrete and immediate reality' of children. Teachers were to have complete control over assessment. There was to be no grade repeating but instead 'recuperative' programmes for under-achievers.[46] Teacher experiment and innovation was given wide opportunity free from outside interference.

The Basic School draws inspiration from Third World examplars, especially Mahatma Gandhi's Basic Education which has been seen internationally as a complete education with a local community orientation for children who would find local employment around the ages of thirteen or fourteen. In Spain this may have had relevance when compulsory schooling only covered the ages six to fourteen and when a substantial proportion of the population worked in agriculture[47] or in the low level service sector in urban centres. It had less relevance as Spain was transformed into an industrial economy in the 1970s and 1980s.

The Basic School curriculum was modified in 1981 when a more conventional list of subjects and suggested content was prescribed. There was a stronger place for subjects seen to be related to the new industrial economy of Spain, especially sciences, 'pre-technological' education and (for the final three years at least) modern languages. Schools were required to offer religious education, from which pupils could withdraw. The Francoist Civics course, with a strong emphasis on patriotism, was dropped.[48] More precise norms of pupil attainment were laid down. Teachers still controlled pupil assessment but they had firmer guidelines on how it should be done.[49]

In 1987 and again in 1989, the structure of the Basic School was challenged in proposals from the Ministry of Education that compulsory schooling should be extended to the age of sixteen and, as a result, it was suggested that primary education should cover six grades (ages 6–12) followed by six grade secondary schooling (ages 12–18).[50]

The six broad objectives were proposed for the new primary school in 1987. They include understanding language (Castillian Spanish and, where appropriate, a regional language) and the ability to use it in expression; encouraging the capacity of pupils to live and work together; elementary knowledge of the physical and social environment; and the development of aesthetic, creative and physical capacities. However, there were also quintessentially encyclopaedist cognitive objectives:

> to develop capacities for observation, discovery, selection, organization and utilization of information; identification of problems in the ambit of their experience; and to begin to acquire habits of objective, ordered and systematic reason.[51]

In effect, development of rational thought was to become a central objective in contrast to the moralism of the Franco period and the somewhat unfocused open curriculum which had replaced it.

Secondary education

The institutes of secondary education established after 1857 paralleled French *lycées* and enrolled pupils at the age of 9 for a 6-year course leading to the *bachillerato* and university entrance (though at an earlier age than in France). The 1970 Education Law had shortened the secondary course to five grades to accommodate the new eight-grade Basic School but altered the curriculum less. There continued to be a core curriculum of Spanish, philosophy and a foreign language but also specialization in literary and scientific branches. Those in the literary branch were encouraged to take mathematics as an option but could not do sciences. The greater literary bias of secondary education in Spain (compared to France or Italy) of the Franco regime was maintained.

Furthermore, upper secondary vocational education was neglected. There were two grades of course equivalent to craft and technician levels. Almost twice as many students opted for the *bachillerato* course compared to vocational options even though some of these had been upgraded to *bachillerato* equivalent and had at least one third of the time devoted to general academic studies.[52]

The modernization of upper secondary education on the contemporary French model was proposed in 1987 and 1989. The range of specializations in the last two grades is to be extended from the literary/scientific division to include human and social sciences, plastic arts, industrial techniques, administrative and management techniques, as well as the older literary-linguistic and science areas.[53] This reflected utilitarian encyclopaedism, especially the belief that general and vocational areas could be united by the common rationality of study in the two areas – particularly the common mathematics and science.

Rational encyclopaedism came through strongly in the objectives of the proposed reform of secondary schooling. Of the 15 listed objectives, the first 7 were concerned largely with the development of rational, systematic thought. Students as a result of the course should be able to: (1) use logical and critical forms of thought; (2) understand the basic elements of scientific method; (3) make use of the main techniques of intellectual work; (4) use fluid and coherent forms of oral and written language; (5) master at least one foreign language; (6) make use of formal languages to solve defined problems; and (7) employ basic theoretical paradigms for the analysis of the physical and/or social world.[54]

The 1987 and 1989 plans also suggested that a standard examination could be developed to determine the award of the *bachillerato*, though continuous teacher assessment would remain at all lower levels. This examination would test knowledge of the basic content and a general capacity for abstraction, organization and synthesis of this content.[55]

Spain has aimed, rather more cogently than France or Italy, at meeting the needs, suggested earlier, for schooling to offer a corpus of rational and systematic knowledge for students and to make some arrangements for the provision of private, sub-cultural and community knowledge.

Two caveats should be made. First, the Spanish style of educational policy-making displays the Don Quixote syndrome. Grand ideals are promulgated, often in legislative form, before the means to achieve them have been established. How far the emphasis on rationality will be accepted will also depend on the behaviour of teachers.

Second, an 'open' curriculum does not necessarily mean that private, individual, and community knowledge that meets non-economic aspirations will be made available. In Spain in the 1980s and beyond, new definitions of local knowledge indeed are overtaking those, based on conventional progressive educational philosophy, which prevailed in the 1970s. These new ideas are associated with the movement towards regional autonomy which has been another central feature of post-Franco Spain.

The 1978 Constitution permitted regional autonomy in educational decision making. As a result, regional languages and cultures have been given a much stronger place in the three most important historic sub-nations of Catalonia, the Basque country and Galicia. In the first two, regionalization has gone further because of the peculiar strengths of these two regions, both of which are industrialized and have levels of wealth much above the average for Spain. So in Catalonia half the population regularly speaks Catalan and the schools since 1978 have offered Catalan teaching for all children who want it. Similar approaches have been taken in the Basque Country where almost a quarter of the population uses Basque. In both these regions, the curriculum has been revised to inject much that reflects local cultures.

The result has been to create sub-national educational systems in two important regions which have, to some extent, sub-national educational cultures. In highly urbanized Catalonia with 15 per cent of the population of Spain, there has been a tradition of private schools teaching Catalan culture which also have been known for their commitment to a child-centred pedagogy. Regional autonomy for Catalonia, and to some extent for the Basque country, has meant that additional local resources have been used to develop these local educational initiatives. So regional cultures in education, unusually in Europe, are associated with a high quality and very well resourced public education system.

In contrast, the other two regions which have full autonomy – Galicia and Andalusia – are poorer and have less powerfully organized regional cultures. Galicia has its own language which has been eroded by centuries of political and economic domination; Andalusia does not have a linguistic-based local culture. The other 11 regions which have partial autonomy, or which have applied for statutes of autonomy, also lack the cultural strengths of Catalonia and the Basque Country and, more significantly, lack their relative wealth. Regionalism may be associated with economic disparities directly affecting educational provision.[56]

There is another weakness of this movement as it affects the kinds of knowledge provided in education. Alternative knowledge cultures are being recognized in education but they are largely political and regionally based. The only other significant sub-culture is that of Catholicism which is reflected in Catholic schools which continue to have government aid but which teach the national curriculum. There is no effective alternative epistemology to underwrite the new sub-cultures of the urban and industrialized society which Spain is becoming.

Portugal

Industrialization, urbanism and, indeed, mass secondary education have not developed sufficiently for their impact on the encyclopaedic curriculum in Portugal to be gauged. The main concern is with quantitative provision rather than with qualitative reorientation. However, the ideals of equality of opportunity and of popular participation have been adopted with varying degrees of vigour by elected governments since the 1974 Revolution.

Portugal is the poorest member state of the European Community. It is a rural society with over a quarter of the workforce engaged in agriculture. Lack of economic development has been associated with the dictatorship of Salazar, 1926–74, which also expressed idealized rustic and Catholic religious values. The Revolution of 1974 brought elected governments which have encouraged industrialization. Though Portugal remains poor, it had the highest rate of economic growth in the European Community in the 1980s.

The period of compulsory schooling was only four years until 1964 when it was expanded to six and schooling was not compulsory for girls until 1960. Even with these restricted legal requirements, there are difficulties in providing universal schooling up to the age of 12 for all children. There is little opportunity for pedagogic innovation in these conditions, especially when subject specialist teachers are used in the two-grade preparatory schools (for children aged 10–12) which follow the four-grade primary schools and when there are many one-teacher schools in the isolated rural areas.[57]

There are two levels of secondary school for the age ranges 12–15 and 15–18, the latter preparing students for university entrance. These schools have followed the traditional patterns of the French *lycée*. Indeed, while Portuguese educational changes have often reflected those of Spain, France is held up as the ideal model, if only to reduce Spanish domination.

A law of 1986 proposed a nine-year period of compulsory schooling in a single and common Basic School for pupils aged 6–15, divided into three cycles. As in Spain and France, the curriculum of the lower secondary cycles consists of the conventional subjects, with some concern for inter-disciplinary themes such as ecology, family, sex, accidents, health, and consumer interests.[58]

Curriculum aims for the Basic School combine the cognitive, individual and social areas which characterize similar levels in France and to some extent Spain. The first objective is:

> to assure a general and common education for all Portuguese which guarantees [pupils opportunities] to discover and develop their interests and aptitudes, capacity for reason, memory and critical spirit, creativity, moral and aesthetic sensibility, prompting individual fulfilment in harmony with the values of social solidarity.[59]

In contrast, the aims of the three-grade, selective upper secondary school (which will combine academic and technical studies) are much more intellectual:

> to assure and develop rationality, reflection and scientific curiosity and to deepen the [understanding] of the basic elements of a humanistic, artistic, scientific and technical culture which constitute cognitive and methodological support, for either further studies or insertion into active life.[60]

As in Spain, educational laws in Portugal are expressions of hope as much as enforceable regulation. Given the major difficulties of educational resources and organization, these aims may not be realized effectively. But the intention to prepare for a more industrialized and urban society through a more rational, scientific and intellectual curriculum is clear. In this, Portugal shares a common interpretation of universal and useful school knowledge with France and Spain.

Portugal has not really faced the question of what other kinds of knowledge are also important. There are proposals for regional autonomy and local participation in schooling but these are made against a tradition of total central control of all aspects of Portuguese education and have not been pursued with great vigour. Sub-cultural identities have not been clarified. Urbanization and industrialization constitute the probable future but not the present in which small agricultural communities are widely spread. Unlike Spain, regional differences are not great except for an imperfectly articulated north-south divide. Portugal has the highest proportion of its population of all European Community countries working abroad, many of whom have since returned, and this diasporic population may have an impact on the definition of Portuguese sub-cultures.

Belgium and Luxembourg
Belgian education has been influenced by French models over a long period of time. Yet Belgium has sharper cultural divisions than any other European Community country which are reflected in a mechanical separation of two distinct education systems. Furthermore there is a 'child-centred' tradition which is distinctive to Belgium.

Belgium is cut in two by a physical frontier which separates French speaking Wallonia and Flemish (Dutch) speaking Flanders. Only Brussels, in Flemish territory, has a significant mixed linguistic population. Historically, power has shifted from one community to another. The French conquest of 1794–1814 was followed by union with the Netherlands. However, independent Belgium since 1830 was dominated initially by the French sector which was the centre of nineteenth-century industrialization. Since 1898, both languages have had equal status in official life.

After 1945 traditional French cultural dominance was reduced further by the growth of new industry in Flanders and the industrial decay of Wallonia. Around 60 per cent of the population is Flemish. The result has been to divide the institutions of the two sectors into almost watertight compartments since the early 1960s. Separate Ministries of Education for the two communities were established in 1968. Elected Flemish and French Cultural Councils which control all aspects of culture were set up during the period of constitutional reforms between 1970 and 1981. The length of compulsory education, the structure of schools and state certificates remained under unified national control.[61]

Two separate education systems mean that every level of educational institution from pre-schooling to universities as well as all aspects of administration are duplicated in the two language areas (the tiny German sector with German medium schools is administered by the Walloons). In practice, there is much in common in the internal organization of the educational institutions of the two language sectors. A national curriculum of objectives, subjects and hours of teaching is issued jointly by the two Cultural Councils.

The historical secularist movement is found in both language communities and it is represented by 'state' schools. Most 'free' schools are Catholic which have a little more than half of all school enrolments and are financed almost completely by public funds. The political unification and secularism on which encyclopaedic education is based in France do not apply in Belgium.

'Child-centred' education in Belgium is associated with the ideas of Ovide Decroly (1871-1932). He was concerned with the relationship between child development – physiological, intellectual and social – and education. He advocated active and individual child learning based on the concept of 'globalization' of the interests and needs of the child. However, the ultimate aims were cognitive, to develop capacities for abstraction and generalization yet giving rein to the need of children to create, imagine and express for themselves.[62]

The child-centred approach in Belgian education is expressed less in an individualization of pedagogy than in a concern for the whole child – physical and emotional as well as intellectual. The official general aims of 1978 give weight to emotional-social issues and suggest that children should be taught to master timidity, anxiety, nervousness and an excessive desire to dominate as well as to deal with social handicaps.[63] Pre-school education in Belgium, perhaps a result of this view, has been the most developed in western Europe.[64] In addition, secondary schools have had for many years psycho-medical units with full-time specialist personnel who are concerned with medical, motivational and intellectual testing of children with the purpose of advising on the most appropriate educational and occupational paths.

Primary education over six grades for 6–12-year-olds is fairly conventional. There is an emphasis on mother tongue and mathematics and the other conventional subjects (including the second language). As in France, there is a focus on achievement in the basic subjects with grade repeating for low attainers.

Secondary education was selective (and similar to old French *lycées*) until 1969 when common secondary schools began to be introduced. Implementation was slow. In the 'renovated' system there is a common course for most pupils in the first two grades (12–14-year-olds) and a standard core curriculum of religious or moral education, mother tongue, a second language, mathematics, study of the human, technical and natural environment, physical education, technological education, art and music with some additional options.[65] There is , however, a remedial stream which follows a restricted curriculum without foreign languages.

Specialization between broad tracks – general, technical and vocational – is quite powerful in the third and fourth grades (14–16-year-olds) and there are subject choices within each track. The common curriculum is relatively limited – only religious or moral education, mother tongue, a second language, human science and physical education. The common curriculum is reduced further in the two-grade upper secondary cycle to religious or moral education, human science and physical education.[66] In practice, students choose three or four subjects from the beginning of the third year of secondary schooling (aged 15) which allows a degree of exclusive specialization not found in most systems of Europe outside Britain.

This differentiation and specialization depart from practice in France. Continuous assessment of pupils by teachers in primary and secondary schools is unchallenged by external examination – even the final certificate which gives entry to higher education is internally assessed. In this respect, Belgium also differs from France, though assessment is carried out by reference to very detailed Ministry guidelines.

The spirit of Belgian education remains encyclopaedic with an emphasis on standardized procedures and the ultimate goal of developing rational thought. The pedagogical choices allowed to parents and teachers are restricted where all possible combinations are detailed by Ministries of Education. The official curricula emphasize rational and critical thought as the primary goal, modified only, in the particular Belgian approach, by a concern for pyscho-pedagogical development of students. The four desired outcomes of secondary education are: the capacity for analysis; the capacity to formulate thoughts clearly and to present a well-structured synthesis; a critical sense; and the capacity for invention or creativity.[67]

Belgium could be grouped with the German Federal Republic and the Netherlands which have an individual and community orientation in education on to which a rational encyclopaedic philosophy is added. But the community orientation in Belgium is restricted rather than enhanced by the rigid politico-linguistic divisions and the individualism is of a limited and peculiar kind. As in Italy and Spain, rationalism remains the highest level goal of education in Belgium even though it is a diluted version of that found in France. The deep cultural rifts in Belgium tend to make the school system conservative rather than innovative.

Education in Luxembourg will be considered very briefly. The very small population means that university and most other forms of higher education are not found inside the country. There are only eight full academic secondary schools. It is difficult to draw many valuable conclusions on the basis of this limited availability of education.

While Luxembourg has been historically under the influence of both Germany and the Netherlands, the school system at both primary and secondary level is predominantly French in organization and curriculum. Or rather it is that of France before 1960 – with surviving lower status secondary schools. This itself indicates a wider currency for French-style education for an indigenous population which must look abroad for higher education and a very large immigrant population (from neighbouring countries and from the main countries outside the European Community which supply the bulk of immigrants in western Europe). The international influences on education in Luxembourg are considerable and a cosmopolitanism has been sought from French educational models.

Conclusion

The organizing assumption of this chapter is that France, Italy, Spain, Portugal, Belgium and Luxembourg are linked by the dominance of a rational encyclopaedic view of school knowledge and a relatively weak place for that which meets individual and community values. This initial proposition mainly stands up. Encyclopaedic universalism does apply generally (though modified in Belgium). Each country has in its curriculum guidelines a strong emphasis upon the development of rational, logical and systematic thought. 'Rational' subjects have a strong place in the national curricula of each of these countries except possibly Belgium.

The pure light of reason shines most brightly in France. Elsewhere it has been obscured by idealist views of knowledge (Italy and, to a lesser extent, Spain) or by individualist perspectives (Belgium). Outside France, rationality is easily debased into factual memorization. The ideal, if not always the achievement of an education which develops a rational intelligence has been maintained in each country. The common currency of rationality is accepted throughout the countries examined.

In some ways more interesting is that, apart from France, each country surveyed in this chapter has gone a considerable way to giving major sub-cultural aspirations an official educational expression. These cultural demands may not be those suggested earlier as the likely outcomes of European economic union. But the intention, if not always the achievement of simultaneously providing for sub-national aspirations and a universal rational knowledge in these countries, apart from France, suggests that the dichotomous 'public' and 'private' curriculum is not unattainable. Ironically, France, the mother of rationality, seems less well equipped to respond to centrifugal knowledge demands than its former cultural disciples.

Chapter Four
Naturalist Variations

In these northern European countries encyclopaedic approaches have been established since the nineteenth century. Yet there are powerful strains of individualist and community knowledge. How far has encyclopaedism, imported from France, developed a sufficient vitality to meet the demand for a youth population trained to think and act rationally? How far have these three countries been able to draw upon their naturalist traditions to meet contemporary private and subcultural aspirations?

The potential for a diversity of educational responses is greatest, perhaps, in the Federal Republic of Germany where individualist pedagogy, a community-work orientation in schooling and a holistic view of knowledge each have strong roots. In contrast, there is a single-mindedness in Dutch and Danish views of community knowledge which allows for fruitful exploration of the boundaries within schools between the public and private curriculum.

The Federal Republic of Germany
The German Federal Republic has the largest population and strongest economy of the nation states of Western Europe. It also has a richer variety of educational traditions than other major European countries. In view of this historic wealth, contemporary practice is disappointing. At most, its admirers can point to the 'completeness and carefulness' of German education which Matthew Arnold noted in the mid-nineteenth century.[1] The German 'Green' party reflects a widely held perception in its claim that German schools 'promote brain-washed citizens and technocrats'.[2] Over the last ten years especially, the German curriculum has been noted for the narrowness of its ambition, however well these limited objectives are achieved.

The context of educational change since 1945

The 'non-reform' of West German education until the 1970s[3] should be put in the context of necessarily cautious politics and a shell-shocked culture which prevailed after the defeat of the Nazis in 1945. Germany, in effect, was under foreign rule from 1945 until 1949 when the Federal Republic was created out of the zones of occupation of the USA, Britain and France. This 'liberation' simply intensified the trauma of separation from the quickly established German Democratic Republic. Furthermore the defeat and the punishment of Germany for the Nazi excesses created in the Federal Republic a culture which eschewed the grand designs of social and political justice which marked the end of the war in Britain and France. Instead, the Germans settled for unspectacular respectability and the hard work which was associated with the 'economic miracle' of industrial regeneration in the 1960s.

Industrial growth centred initially on the pre-war chemicals, iron and steel, and engineering in the Ruhr but diversified into high-technology manufacture in the south from the mid-1970s. However much the Germans tried to insulate politics, culture and society from the effects of economic success, there were inevitably social implications. Immigration into the Federal Republic, particularly by Turkish, Yugoslav and Greek workers to meet labour shortages from the 1960s, was the highest of all the major European countries (at around 7 per cent of the total population).

Political responses to the social aspirations created by economic growth were not apparent until after 1969 when a Social Democrat government began to initiate reform. The political programme was preceded by a revolt of university students in the late 1960s which was a stimulant to educational change in the early 1970s.[4] However, the pace of political reform slowed down after the industrial recession in the later 1970s and the election of a Christian Democrat government in 1982, which has returned to the caution of the 1950s and early 1960s.

High culture was perhaps an even greater force in nineteenth-century Germany than in Britain or France. It had been destroyed to a large extent by the Nazis and was not able to re-invigorate itself after 1945 in conditions of German political and cultural self-effacement. So this high culture, based partly on the universities, was not able to set goals for the rest of the education system as it did in Britain and France.

There were two main results for education of the retreat of high culture and the lack of ambitious political programmes. Access was opened up later than in other major European countries. Economic organizations which grew so much in power and self-confidence in the economic miracle – especially employers – were able to get a leverage on educational policy and practice that was not matched in other European countries.

Changing school and changing curriculum
Whereas in most other European countries the main pressure for change in the school curriculum has been the democratization of secondary education, the Federal Republic of Germany has retained a selective system. Yet, within the tripartite organization of secondary schooling, there have been increased pressures for higher standards of individual student achievement.

Primary schools
German primary schools have oscillated between uniformity and externality on the one side and child-centredness and a community orientation on the other. State elementary schooling has been universally provided in some parts of Germany since the seventeenth century and was compulsory in Prussia – the largest of the pre-unification states of Germany – since 1717. Universal provision was impelled by Lutheran Protestantism and the continuing link between school attendance and Christian belief. The uniformity imposed by the Bible as a standard text was reinforced by the order of Prussian militarism in the early and mid-nineteenth century, when the schoolmaster was likened to the drill-sergeant and his effectiveness in training future infantrymen was claimed to be the basis for the Prussian victory over the French at the Battle of Sedan in 1870.

Yet the German elementary school was also intimately linked with the organic rural community in the minds of early nineteenth-century German nationalists. It was supposed to reflect the concrete, tactile and emotional experience of the immediate community as much as to transmit external knowledge. German location of the roots of their culture in a mystical relationship with forests and mountains grounds the elementary school in a naturalist setting as much as the philosophy of the many German progressive educationists.

The primary school after 1945 reverted largely to uniformity rather than to romantic naturalism. A separate *Grundschule* for 6–10-year-olds replaced the older all-through *Volksschule* as some kind of secondary education became available for all children. The achievement orientation was encouraged by the short length of primary schooling in years as well as the short (morning only) school day. Outside West Berlin and Bremen, where primary schooling has six grades, the four year *Grundschule* offers very little time for preparation and selection for secondary education. The development of pre-school education in the 1970s, so that 90 per cent of 5-year-olds and 65 per cent of 4-year-olds were in kindergartens in 1982,[5] has not changed this orientation.

The primary school curriculum emphasizes language and computation. First grade children (6–7-years-old) spend only 18 hours a week in school but 14 of these hours are devoted to language and arithmetic and only 4 hours to aesthetic and physical education. Grades 2-4 (7–10 years-old) spend around 11 hours a week on German, 5 or 6 on mathematics, 2 on religious education and further time on introducing the subjects of secondary education such as social studies and, in some cases, a modern language. Though these older children have 25 hours of classes a week, they spent little more than about 4 hours a week on art, music and physical education.

Curriculum prescriptions are made by *Länder* authorities. However, they are not as full as those applying in secondary education. The greatest restriction is the very systematic assessment that occurs before then. Teacher assessment of individual pupils is required by each *Länd* and there are national scales.[6] Each pupil is given a numerical grade (1–6) twice a year by the class teacher on the basis of tests and day-to-day class work. This grade is communicated to parents (and indeed has been challenged in the courts). Grades determine selection to secondary education. The proportions going to the academic schools (*Gymnasien*) have risen from 15 per cent in the 1960s to 28 per cent in the late 1980s.[7] Yet over 50 per cent of parents would like their children to go to the *Gymnasium* and gain the *Abitur*.[8] Though parent wishes have an influence on selection, the grades are paramount.

Achievement targets do not mean that child-centredness is totally absent from German primary schools. There is much pedagogy which is relaxed, open and child-orientated. It can be found in the typical primary schools where whole class teaching, the use of prescribed texts and the dominance of assessment does not prevent the use of attractive materials and emphasis on child movement and discovery.[9] Even the prescribed texts can be rich and colourful while real objects are used as much as possible in mathematics and science.

More thoroughgoing child-centred teaching is peripheralized. It may be confined to experiments in more 'progressive' *Länder* which are offered as 'optional' schools. So, for instance, the 'Jena' plan of Peter Peterson – which involves individual and small group learning and discovery by primary school children, with the consequent disappear-

ance of the traditional timetable and even divisions between grades –
was extended from 'optional' schools to all primary education in the
largest *Land* of North-Rhine Westphalia in 1985.[10] This change may not
be adopted in practice as widely as was hoped but it indicates a
continuing reaction against uniformity. Similarly, the private school
movement is patronized by parents less in the hope of gaining social
distinction for their children than because the private schools –
especially the Waldorf-Steiner type – offer a more child-centred
pedagogy.[11] Yet these private schools, despite part financing by the *Land*
governments, cater for only 5 per cent of children.

Secondary education

The survival of selection has not buried the issue of equality of
opportunity either for politicians or for individual parents. The
accommodation of demands for equal opportunities has led to
standardization of the core curriculum between different types of
secondary school and to an emphasis on examinations and assessment
to allow transfers from one kind of secondary education to another.

The tripartite system consists of academic *Gymnasien* leading to
higher education entry after nine years (grades 5–13). The *Realschulen*
are technical schools with their own kind of leaving certificate after six
years (grades 5–10) while the *Hauptschulen* have the lowest status,
contain the highest proportion of the age group and offer five years
(grades 5–9) which is extended to six grades in some *Länder* and leads
to its own leaving certificate. Comprehensive schools (*Gesamtschulen*)
are found in some *Länder* and exist alongside the tripartite system.

The Gymnasium – traditional and contemporary

Like the French *lycée* the German *Gymnasium* was born as a state
school out of military reconstruction. William von Humboldt, who
reformed these schools after the defeat of Prussia by Napoleon in 1806,
had a humanist ideal for the new *Gymnasien*. He believed that the study
of the literature, history and philosophy of ancient Greece and Rome
was the means to create a moral and cultivated politico-administrative
élite.[12]

Even in the nineteenth century, the humanist rationale was never
allowed, as it was in England, to demean the importance of mathematics and science. It was believed that scientific knowledge should be
mastered in the continuing search for total understanding.[13] By the end
of the nineteenth century there had been a moderate shift towards the
study of the sciences in the *Gymnasium*.[14] Encyclopaedic universalism

had penetrated the *Gymnasium* even in the nineteenth century, since it provided the broad base of study which was seen as necessary for entry to the philosophy faculty of the university.

From the early nineteenth century the *Gymnasium* has been a state school with a curriculum regulated by the Ministries of Education. Its teachers were appointed and controlled by the state. Its students prepared for the state examination – the *Abitur* – which gave entry to university. State control seems to have been linked to consistently high standards. Sir Michael Sadler's reports of 1898, which compared the *Gymnasium* with equivalent English schools, suggested that the intellectual achievements of the *Gymnasium* were noticeably better – a view which had been anticipated earlier by Matthew Arnold.[15]

There were two facets of this superiority. The majority of pupils achieved highly in a wide range of subjects in contrast to England where intellectual high-achievers were a minority. Second, there was a parity of standards between schools that was not matched in England. The picture was so depressing for Sadler that he was forced to emphasize the moral and individualist qualities of English public schools that were not equalled in Germany and also to suggest that the English tended to catch up in 'the great and searching examination of actual life'.[16]

In the nineteenth century different *Gymnasien* had specialized in particular fields. This continued when the *Gymnasium* was reformed as a result of an agreement between *Länder* ministers in 1955 – the three types then became Classical, Modern Language and Mathematics/Science. Furthermore, the numbers of *Gymnasien* were expanded to include all schools which prepared pupils for university entrance – the basic criterion of *Gymnasium* status.

The *Gymnasium*, despite changes after 1955, remains an academic school with a heavy bias towards language study. Indeed what distinguishes the *Gymnasium* from other kinds of secondary education is not only the nine-year course but the insistence on the study of three languages other than German in Classical and Modern Language *Gymnasien* compared to two in the Science *Gymnasien*, one or two in the *Realschule* and one in the *Hauptschule*.[17]

The intention in reforming the *Gymnasium* in 1955 was largely conservative. It was to put the seal on successful resistance to the attempt in 1947 of the Allied Control Council of the American, Soviet, British and French occupying forces to decree a comprehensive high school on the American (or Soviet) model.[18] The result was the preservation of an academic and selective school with an encyclopaedic curriculum.

Three major developments have modified the character of the *Gymnasium* since the early 1970s. First, a completely common curriculum for the first two grades of all types of secondary school was introduced in 1976 to allow correction of mistakes in selection at the end of primary education.[19] So the *Gymnasium* curriculum for the first six years diverges from that of other secondary schools only from the third grade and then simply in that more time is devoted to foreign languages and the level of treatment is expected to be more advanced that in the other kinds of school.

Second, the *Gymnasium* is losing an exclusively academic orientation through parent and student choice. Increasing proportions of the age group are entering the *Gymnasien*. Furthermore, larger numbers of *Gymnasium* pupils do not see it as a route to higher education. Between 20 and 30 per cent of *Gymnasium* students take the *Realschule* leaving examination at the end of the sixth grade and then leave, and around 30 per cent of those completing the full *Gymnasium* course and gaining the *Abitur* go on to work rather than university.[20]

The third development centres upon the upper secondary course – grades 11–13 in the *Gymnasium*. Traditionally students were examined in 13 subjects for the *Abitur*. In 1972 the *Länder* ministers agreed to a new system which would allow more specialization and student choice. Students must follow at least one course in each group consisting of languages (German and foreign), social studies, and sciences. But a distinction is made between basic and main courses. The latter are studied at a more specialized level and have a greater weight than the basic courses in the final *Abitur* examination. This has allowed some students to spend much time on what are regarded by many as soft options such as sport or sociology.[21] Yet this specialization does not permit students to drop studies in any of the main areas, especially languages and mathematics/sciences at any time in the nine-year course.

The continuous assessment of students means that around 20 per cent have to repeat a grade at some point of the *Gymnasium* course.[22] Serious failures have to drop to other kinds of school. Within the schools, there is little streaming or setting by attainment. But the achievement orientation tends to focus study upon testable areas such as languages and mathematics.

The heavy intellectual diet is appropriate primarily for specialized university studies, which themselves have attracted considerable criticism in the Federal Republic. There are demands that the whole nine-year course should be reduced by a year[23] which would bring it into line with other European countries and allow university graduates to start work a year younger. The *Gymnasium* is seen by many as peripheral to the German society and economy though the critics diverge widely on what they believe should be done.

The Realschule, Hauptschule and Gesamtschule

These three kinds of schools were created out of an agreement between *Länder* Ministers of Education at Hamburg in 1964. The new system was very similar – in surface appearance – to the state secondary schools prevailing in England and Wales. So the *Gymnasium* could be equated with the grammar school, the *Realschule* with the secondary technical school, the *Hauptschule* with the secondary modern school and the *Gesamtschule* with the comprehensive school. However, the parallels can be misleading. The *Realschule* is much more central to German secondary schooling than the ill-fated secondary technical school was in England and it is supported by elements of an historic German culture that have few parallels in England.

Realschulen, which emphasized the study of mathematics and science rather than classics and which prepared students for work rather than university, had almost as long and distinguished a history as the *Gymnasien*. The original *Realschulen* were largely converted into *Gymnasien* with modern language or mathematics/science orientations after 1945. The post-1964 *Realschulen* were created from Prussian middle schools which had been established in 1872.[24] The re-created *Realschulen* rapidly took on the same character, rationale and attractiveness of their nineteenth-century namesakes.

Realschulen provide six years of secondary schooling up to the age of 16 (grades 5–10). Their students grew rapidly in numbers from 1964 so that they accounted for 18 per cent of all secondary enrolments in 1969. By 1986, the proportion had risen to 29 per cent.[25] The *Realschulen* are attractive to students and their parents because they are seen to prepare for technician-level jobs in expanding industry rather than interminable university education. The robust traditional view that the *Gymnasium* was for a cultivated but marginal élite has been reinforced by recent high levels of unemployment among university graduates.[26]

Realschule teachers have been largely university graduates of the same standing as their colleagues in *Gymnasien*. Its curriculum is largely the same as that of the *Gymnasium* for the equivalent grades except that no classical languages are studied and a second foreign language (usually French) is optional and additional to the one compulsory foreign language (usually English). The electives in the *Realschule* do include also general education courses with a vocational bias such as business mathematics, commercial English or industrial economics. Yet there is an overall emphasis on the subjects of the core curriculum which gives a sufficient status to the leaving certificate for its holders to enter grade 11 of the *Gymnasium* or a higher-level vocational school. The *Realschule* does not have the tag of failure associated with non-élite secondary education in other systems.

In contrast, the *Hauptschulen* have struggled to escape from the dead-end image. Like short-cycle, unselective secondary schools in other countries the *Hauptschulen* emerged from the upper grades of the old extended elementary school. The course is 5 years up to the age of 15 (Grades 5–9) though increasing numbers of students stay on to the end of Grade 10 which is now compulsory in some *Länder*. Its teachers, in the past, have been prepared in institutions below university level. They would teach a range of subjects to one class. The original guidelines emphasized practical experience in not only such subjects as craft, which had a prominent place, but they had also had much more limited ambitions of knowledge coverage in the academic areas.

Over time the *Hauptschule* curriculum has become much more achievement orientated, especially in mathematics and science. A foreign language (usually English) has been made compulsory. There is streaming between classes on the basis of achievement to a degree not found in the *Gymnasium* or the *Realschule*. The result is a core curriculum for upper streams which is largely common with the other types of secondary school.

Considerable attention has been given in other countries to the vocational orientation element of the *Hauptschule* curriculum – *Arbeitslehre*. This subject was introduced as part of the compulsory curriculum of the *Hauptschule* in 1969 and takes up three or four hours a week. It includes work experience as well as the study of technical and industrial life in order to help pupils to understand 'economic' society and to choose the most appropriate occupations. It is highly regarded in the Federal Republic and there are proposals to extend it to other forms of secondary education.[27]

Arbeitslehre is marginal rather than the jewel in the crown of the *Hauptschule* curriculum. The major emphasis for students and teachers is work in academic subjects including German, English and social studies as well as mathematics and science which lead to the *Hauptschule* leaving certificate. This qualification gives access to higher levels of education either in the *Gymnasium* or in the vocational sector. More crucially it is the *sine qua non* for admission to an apprenticeship. Employers' insistence on the *Hauptschule* certificate has not only given the *Hauptschule* an academic achievement orientation but, it is claimed, has led to significantly higher standards of attainment among *Hauptschule* students than their equivalents in Britain.[28]

Despite relatively high standards of achievement in academic areas, there is concern about the 10 per cent of the total age group who leave the *Hauptschule* without a certificate and fail to make good this deficiency in a vocational school. This new 'under-class' may be smaller in numbers than in other European countries but it is a significant proportion of *Hauptschule* students. The marginalized unemployable class is seen to be a responsibility of the *Hauptschule*.

The establishment of comprehensive *Gesamtschulen* was also agreed by the *Länder* ministers in 1964 – and had been urged by the American occupying forces in the late 1940s. But these schools take only 5 per cent of the age group and are significant only in West Berlin (20 per cent). They have been opposed by the Christian Democrat/ Christian Social governments of Bavaria and Baden-Wurttemberg which have not only refused to develop comprehensive schooling in their areas but have prevented it from becoming recognized as an official alternative to the tripartite system in federal policy.

The Federal Republic's tripartite system was able to win political and popular acceptance only when it could be demonstrated that assignment to one kind of school at the age of ten did not irredeemably close doors of opportunity. The *Realschule* and particularly the *Hauptschule* were forced to aim at levels of achievement for most students which were not obviously inferior to those of other schools. Apart from the 10 per cent of the age group who fail to gain any recognized educational or vocational qualifications, this aim seems to have been achieved more effectively than in most other European countries.

The cost has been high. Complaints about the alienation of students from school, about listlessness, too much pressure and a 'dehumanizing' curriculum have increased. The achieving school has been too successful and is producing students who are hostile to the achievement ethic.

The place of the naturalist and child-centred traditions then become more relevant – and possibly also the place of the traditional humanist aims. Achievement in the common core curriculum of secondary education leads to the naturalist education of the workplace and the humanist education of the university. Does this articulation have real meaning and purpose and what place is there for naturalist and child-centred education within secondary schooling?

There are also questions about whether the standards of achievement in themselves have any meaning or relevance. The core curriculum of secondary schools emphasizes the acquisition of universal standard knowledge. Subjects such as mathematics, science and languages with logical structures which can be methodically and systematically mastered predominate in the core curriculum. In this sense it is encyclopaedist. But does it give enough stress to the development of rationality which is central to the French conception of worthwhile knowledge?

Curriculum issues and debates

What common curriculum?
It is ironic that in the Federal Republic the achievement ethos – the goal of 'quality' – which is expressed in explicit and systematic testing of pupils, is accompanied by a collective self-doubt about the purpose of knowledge transmission and acquisition. English ideals of 'moral sensibility' and the French goal of 'rational intelligence' are paralleled in Germany by little more than 'thoroughness'. Debate about education over the last ten years has become hyperbolic with predictions of 'catastrophe' in a purposeless system.[29]

Originally the three types of secondary school were each associated with one arm of the triangle of total German epistemology. The *Gymnasium* would be humanist – or, at least would prepare for the humanist university – the *Realschule* encyclopaedic and the *Hauptschule* naturalist. In practice, they have converged towards a uniform encyclopaedism.

The encyclopaedist dominance is associated with the central position of four subjects in the lower secondary core curriculum – German, mathematics, science and English. This core consists of content which may be systematically and methodically arranged. But it does not meet student aspirations regarding knowledge, as is revealed in their choice of individually more congenial alternatives in the last three grades of the *Gymnasium*.

These core subjects do have a rational content and their teaching in German secondary schools does emphasize the understanding of structures and logical connections. For German teachers and students, like their counterparts in France, mathematics is about grasping algorhythmic structures and logical exercises – most frequently worked by teachers and pupils together in a whole class setting. Science – especially when it divides into physics, chemistry and biology around the middle of the secondary school – is also about the understanding of theories, rules and structures. English observers have criticized it because there is not enough practical student experience, observation and experiment.[30] But, like the French, German science teaching is about providing students with means to organize the world intellectually in an overt and systematic way rather than assuming that unmediated practical experience produces comprehension à la Archimedes.

Languages – whether German or foreign – combine a study of grammar with an emphasis on learning how to use the language in a structured way, whether in speech or writing. Creative writing may have little place[31] and grammar may be overestimated. But the ultimate aim is to encourage students to become competent working architects of both written and spoken language, of both the popular and classical varieties. The aim may be to produce language technicians rather than poets, but language theory is firmly wedded to and indeed clearly subordinated to language practice.[32]

Yet German encyclopaedism is an inferior version of a French model. Rationalism is not so central to German conceptions of ultimate knowing and thinking as it is to the French. The universalist principle becomes predominant. The knowledge diet is expanded continuously. This may be illustrated by reference to the teaching of German literature where the detail of textual analysis has become so intense that students have little conception of the overall patterns of German literary achievement – as German writers such as Gunter Grass have complained.[33]

The weakness of the encyclopaedic approach in Germany may be that Germans follow Plato literally. At the highest levels reason is subordinated to intelligent insight into the nature of humanity. Rationality in the schools is simply a means to an end which will be accomplished in humanist universities. In another way, rationality is a means to an end. The acquisition of methodical and structured knowledge can be tested reliably. Rigorous testing of quality ultimately degrades the quality it is testing.

Vocational relevance

The Federal Republic of Germany is often held up in other countries, especially Britain, as the model to emulate in steering compulsory schooling to vocational preparation and the world of work. In many ways the Federal Republic deserves this admiration for its effective system of vocational preparation and most particularly for its success in motivating young people to accept it. But this admiration should be tempered in two ways. First, the need for schools to prepare for work is very widely accepted in German historic culture. It runs with rather than against popular aspirations in contrast to many other countries. Second, the link between school and vocational training is now being threatened by the academic achievement ethos in general school education which itself reflects new demands of work.

The historic work culture of Germany is highly important. Marx's concept of work as alienation has been internalized much more fully in Britain than in his native Germany. For Germans, any kind of work has dignity and responsibility – in effect, it is a vocation as in the traditional English sense of the word. So work is a moral activity and, indeed, for some prominent late nineteenth- and early twentieth-century advocates of work-orientated education such as Kerschensteiner and Eduard Spranger, vocational education should be the basis of citizenship.

These values have been translated into educational theory and practice through the assumption that 'occupation is the medium of education'.[34] Curriculum and pedagogy therefore should aim at replicating real work as nearly as possible within schools. This concept has been adopted in the progressive school movement – especially the Waldorf schools. It was central to the continuation schools which Kerschensteiner set up as Director of Education for Bavaria in the first decade of the twentieth century.[35] He believed that practical work in schools should be real craft reflecting contemporary industrial life rather than artificial or purely decorative and recreational activities, if it was to achieve its moral and civic purposes.[36] Work becomes a culture and its reflection in the school curriculum in turn brings a wider culture into the school.

In practice, the *Hauptschule* and the *Realschule*, it has been noted, have had a vocational orientation to some subjects of study. Its highest contemporary expression, however, remains *Arbeitslehre*, which has excited admiration in other countries. Yet *Arbeitslehre* may be an exception to the general trend of German secondary education where academic study in the *Realschule* and the *Hauptschule* is squeezing out vocationally orientated subjects. The national association of manual craft employers has complained that the *Hauptschule* has become too academic and neglects basic craft training – including the development of pupils 'own creative faculties' that it carried out in the past.[37] Yet it is employers themselves who insist upon high general academic achievement of their apprentices.

Vocational relevance is achieved largely in the post-compulsory vocational schools. Of these, the continuation schools – *Berufsschulen* – have by far the most students. Indeed, attendance for one day or two days a week at the *Berufsschulen* is legally compulsory for all young workers below the age of 18. The general education content follows Kershensteiner's original idea with considerable emphasis on social, civic and moral education. Besides basic German, mathematics and science the curriculum includes social studies, with an orientation towards the social context of working life, as well as religious education.[38] In some ways, then, *Arbeitslehre* was an extension downwards of the *Berufsschule* into the *Hauptschule*.

There is an increasing separation of the technical craft training and the general education elements of apprenticeship training. Employers are emphasizing in-plant craft training of a complex nature. The examinations for the craft elements are controlled by trade associations which award the final certificates. The general elements of the continuation school curriculum are being marginalized.

Higher level vocational education has expanded. Apart from the full-time equivalent of the *Berufsschule*, there are also institutions providing technician-level training which demand the *Realschule* certificate for entry and which also give general education (German, social studies, mathematics, science and a modern language) as well as technical studies leading to a certificate which gives entry to higher education. The movement to higher-grade technical education parallels similar developments in other industrial countries.

If it were possible to pick the ideal culture in which to establish vocationally orientated education, then the Federal Republic would have among the strongest claims. Yet the vocational-general education link in the Republic is weakening as elsewhere. This separation seems to be less a product of a declining work ethic in a younger generation (though this may be a factor) than the result of changes in the skills demanded in modern manufacture. Employers in the Republic have found that their future workers are best trained by an initial high level of general education followed by complex, intensive but specific training on the job. This is the product of changes in technology and has little to do with the success or failure of the school system in giving their pupils a vocational orientation.

Individualism

There has been vigorous political debate in the last twenty years over the rights of students, parents and communities to a choice of educational knowledge. Elements of the 'left' have attacked the 'dehumanizing' character of state education. The 'right' have equated greater student choice with declining standards and moral laxity. The

left have pressed for a greater concern for individual interests at every
level of the education system. The right have focused their attack
particularly upon the relative freedom of curriculum which was
introduced in Grades 11–13 of the *Gymnasium* in 1972.

Individual choice, whether for students, parents or communities, was
established traditionally at certain key points of German education. In
universities, students have enjoyed *Freiheit des Studiums*. This means
that each student can construct his or her own individual programme,
picking the individual elements from any area or even university that
they wish, since students traditionally have moved from university to
university. The student chooses when to offer himself or herself for
examination and nominates the examiners. One consequence of this
freedom has been that the average length of time a student in the mid-
1980s took to complete the first degree was almost seven years. The
philosophy behind this practice is that the university is a centre of
research and even the first year student is a free scholar. Though
freedom of university students has been modified in a number of ways
in recent years, the broad principle survives.

Freiheit des Studiums has had no application in *Gymnasien*. Indeed
the freedom of *Abitur* holders to enrol in any faculty of any university
was an argument for a highly standardized *Gymnasium* course. From
1972, student choice moved, in a very limited way, into the upper classes
of the *Gymnasium* in that students could choose their main (advanced)
courses from a wide range of options.

It was attacked by political parties, employers and *Gymnasium*
teachers with the result that regulations were changed in 1987 to give
greater weight in the final assessment to the compulsory basic courses
and especially studies in German, mathematics and modern languages.[39] Individual choice is not acceptable in phases of education
which lead to state examinations whose validity and comparability
across *Länder* have become a central element of faith for some
participants in educational debate.

Student alienation from school became an issue in German schools
in the late 1970s and early 1980s[40] just as it has been in Britain, France
and other countries. While the political 'right' has generally responded
by calling for a return to traditional standards which they saw as
threatened by general permissiveness in schools, the 'left' has argued for
a curriculum which takes more account of individual children and
indeed, youth values. In part the battle over Peace Education in schools
in 1983–4 reflected this difference. The 'left' generally felt that the
curriculum should reflect the peace orientation of youth culture while

the 'right' insisted upon proper recognition of the role of the security forces in defending German Federal Republic.[41]

Outside the main political debate, parents have complained about excessive pressure of attainment targets and the core curriculum upon children.[42] More generally there have been demands for a stronger pastoral function for schools (and German teachers, unlike their counterparts in France, have traditionally had a pastoral role). These demands suggest the need for stronger attention to the all-round development of individual pupils.

German education has an individualist tradition which is stronger, for instance, than that of France. Teachers do habitually develop close and sympathetic relations with individual children. Practical experience is drawn upon wherever possible in teaching.

The degree to which teaching is permitted to start from the all-round interests of children is determined by geographical location. Child-centred approaches are much more possible for teachers to adopt in northern Social Democrat *Länder* – especially in the city states of West Berlin, Hamburg and Bremen – than in the Christian Democrat south. Yet the achievement ethos is embedded also in Social Democrat thinking because it is aligned to equality of opportunity as much as in Christian Democrat concern for traditional standards and industrial efficiency. The prevalence of this ethos almost inevitably reduces opportunities for individual interests.

Sub-cultural and community interests
The core curriculum gives little opportunity for the reflection of sub-cultural interests in the content of schooling. Though the Federal Republic has the largest immigrant population of the larger countries of Europe, relatively few concessions have been made to immigrant cultures except for the notorious Turkish medium schools of Bavaria, which were seen as part of a strategy of denying residence rights to the families of immigrant workers.[43] Apart from this, only limited experiments have been introduced, notably in West Berlin, to permit Turkish as the first foreign language of secondary education.[44] The overall tendency was to uniformity even for students from cultural minorities.

This standardization of curriculum and student learning objects takes place against a traditional German respect for the culture of the home. The Federal Republic shares with other countries in Northern Europe – including Denmark within the European Community and the USSR outside it – a half-day school pattern. School begins at 8 am and

ends between 12.30 and 2 pm (depending on the age of children). The
rationale is that school should not intrude too much into the wider
social – especially familial – educative environment of children.
Morning-only school is still secure, with only a very small number of
experimental all-day schools. The most popular form of all-day school
is one in which the afternoon is concerned exclusively with recreation.[45]
So the assembly line school is still firmly relegated to a limited part of
the total child experience.

How far a child-centred and community orientation develops in the
Federal Republic's education system depends to a large extent on the
changes in German cultural aspirations. The achievement ethic which
dominated education after 1945 largely derived from the ambition to
reconstruct German society by hard work – to which was added the
vision of providing social opportunities for those willing to show the
right application.

The possible revolt against technocratic society and against the
dominance of the work ethic does have some cultural bases for success.
A revival of individualism, however, is likely to have greatest success in
certain locations in the Federal Republic where the local political
climate is favourable to a revival of long-standing individualist and
small-group traditions in German culture.

The Netherlands and Denmark

In these countries, local community and parent participation in
education have been institutionalized over time much more powerfully
than in the Federal Republic of Germany or elsewhere in the European
Community. How far have these participatory traditions permitted the
development of a curriculum which respects the private knowledge
aspirations of individuals and communities? How far has the methodical, rationalist universalism of the encyclopaedic tradition been
retained and reconciled with this naturalism?

In the Netherlands, an institutional pluralism has prevailed which
respects the autonomy of different religious and social groups in
education and other areas of public life. From this, parental choice has
become paramount and individualist teaching has developed. Denmark, by contrast, has had a high level of social cohesion based on rural
community values which have had a powerful impact on education.
The populist movements which have challenged encyclopaedic centralism differ in the two countries.

The Netherlands

Dutch pluralism is explained in terms of a multi-pillared society. Each group has developed and retained its own public institutions in separation from the others. Yet this particularism has been accommodated in one national state and one national culture through the development of an ethos of mutual co-existence. There is also an internationalism of outlook in the Netherlands expressed as a tolerance of other national cultures which has been impelled by the historical pre-eminence of the Netherlands in international trade and by the need for a nation with a little known national language to communicate with powerful neighbouring states.

The multi-pillared society is based historically upon religion. Catholics and Protestants, in the past, have been almost equally balanced in numbers. The growth of secularism since the early nineteenth century has produced a contemporary situation where roughly 35 per cent of the population is Catholic, 30 per cent Protestant and 35 per cent secular. Traditionally each group was self-contained and had its own separate institutions such as trade unions, schools, newspapers and sports teams. Marriage and even friendship across these boundaries were rare.

The pillars operated economic activities and were mirrored in social class divisions. The idea of social classes as vertical pillars meant that there was less expectation of social mobility than in other European societies.[46] Yet there has also been a tolerance of other social groups which has not been found in other divided societies. Harmony, accommodation and mutual respect have prevailed. This has been extended to allow a legitimate identity to other groups – whether immigrants from former colonies such as Indonesia or the Surinam and the Antilles or alternative sub-cultures – though those groups which have an element of identifiable Dutchness such as Indonesians are welcomed more than those who appear alien like the Caribbean immigrants.[47] Accommodation has been encouraged further by the positive social welfare policies of successive governments since 1945 towards the disadvantaged.

State and state-aided education is pluralist. Since 1848, each religious group has been permitted almost total autonomy in running its own schools and since 1917 these 'private' institutions have had all their recurrent expenditure met by the government. As a result, substantial proportions of primary and secondary school and higher education enrolments are in institutions controlled by Catholic or Protestant religious bodies. But public support for private schools is not confined to the churches. Any group of parents can apply for state support for a private school. Pluralism extends also into decentralization of control over state schools with local authorities having considerable power, including the inspection of schools. Furthermore, since 1970, school Participation Councils have been introduced which permit considerable parent involvement in individual school policy-making.[48]

Pluralism operates also in a more socially conservative way. Secondary schools for children aged 12 years 6 months and above are differentiated into five types with different lengths of course. There are selective examinations at the end of primary schooling for the two most prestigious types of secondary school. As in the German Federal Republic, there is an assumption of social and occupational differentiation which schools can initiate on perceptions of pupil ability as well as on parental choice. Also as in the Federal Republic the common secondary school is an experimental institution for a small minority.

Curriculum and curriculum change
In view of the various levels of differentiation of secondary schools on the one hand and the institutional pluralism and decentralism on the other, it may be surprising that a centralized and encyclopaedic curriculum has remained secure in the Netherlands. The national Ministry of Education determines the main elements of a national curriculum including the core subjects for each grade of schooling. Examinations at the end of the four main types of secondary education include compulsory subjects and nationally uniform written papers as well as school assessment.

The subjects of the national core curriculum for secondary schools are similar to those of equivalent schools in the German Federal Republic. The main difference is a greater emphasis in the Netherlands on languages and correspondingly less on mathematics and sciences. Students in the two kinds of high status secondary education – the six grade *VWO* (similar to the German *Gymnasium*) and the five grade *HAVO* (like the German *Realschule*) – take two or three foreign languages throughout the course, which may include Latin and/or Greek in the classical forms of *VWO*.

The final examinations of the *VWO* and *HAVO* allow a degree of specialization in either languages/social studies or mathematics/sciences which is paralleled in neither the German Federal Republic nor France. The seven-subject examination in the past for the language/social studies section had to include Dutch and two or three foreign (classical or modern) languages together with one or two of history, geography and economics. So mathematics and science was not compulsory in the language/social studies section. In the mathematics/science streams, two languages, mathematics or one or two sciences have been compulsory but not social studies.

The unselective four-grade schools (*MAVO* and *LAVO*), which are similar to the Federal Republic's *Hauptschule*, stream pupils by attainment and the top group prepares for an examination similar to that of *HAVO* schools. Lower streams follow a more restricted curriculum and are assessed internally as the basis for the leaving certificate. There are also lower-status secondary schools which provide two years of general education followed by two years of vocational studies with a craft orientation.[49]

Standardization is weaker in secondary schooling in the Netherlands than in the German Federal Republic. Lower-attaining students are not under the same pressure as their German counterparts to achieve by uniform measures. There is a limited space for a humanist orientation in some academic specializations leading on to those universities which have a humanist orientation in the tradition of Erasmus. There is a degree of early vocational specialization in some schools.

Yet these variations upon the encyclopaedic tradition do not reflect the conscious adoption of an alternative epistemology so much as the intrusion of the 'pillared' society in the education system. A society which is so strongly partitioned vertically according to religion, race and social class perhaps naturally has adopted an education system with similar impermeable boundaries. In these conditions, it is not the minor breaches of encyclopaedism which are remarkable but the strength of the survival of an encyclopaedic core of studies.

However, Dutch education does deviate from encyclopaedic universalism in primary schooling. Considerable opportunity for school-level curriculum decision-making has been introduced in the 1970s and 1980s. This has occurred against the background of the survival of legally prescribed subjects of study. The 1985 Primary Education Act reaffirmed the approaches of its predecessors of 1920 and 1970 in producing a list of required subjects: Dutch, mathematics, English, history, geography, religion or 'ideological studies', health education, social studies, sciences, music, crafts, physical education and movement. Indeed the compulsory subjects were extended in 1985 to include English and permission was given to introduce Frisian in Friesland and the mother tongues of non-Dutch children as subjects or media of instruction.[50]

The 1985 Act extended throughout the country experiments which had been operating in certain areas and schools since the 1950s. Individual schools can draw up their own curriculum plans which allow cross-subject or integrated projects, individual or small-group teaching, permeability of year groups and opportunities for individual children to work at their own pace.[51]

School-level innovations must be documented in advance in school curriculum plans, which are submitted to inspectors who determine whether they satisfy the national curriculum prescriptions. And greater flexibility of approaches to teaching and learning does not mean that encyclopaedic system and method are abandoned. In practice there is still much emphasis on teacher-centred whole-group oral interaction, especially in language and mathematics, to ensure that children collectively acquire basic principles in the traditional encyclopaedic fashion.[52]

The child-centred primary school curriculum has been made possible by the extension of the primary cycle downwards so that it now covers children aged 4–12. It has been helped by the very active involvement of parents in the running of schools which has encouraged the development of a school-centred curriculum. This participation itself derives from fundamental social patterns in the Netherlands.

Yet encyclopaedic standardization remains. It may be weak in that it lacks the over-arching rationalism of France and the central language-mathematics axis of the Federal Republic of Germany. But there is no apparent epistemological alternative. The weakening of encyclopaedism is a reflection of the strength of socio-political particularism and participation in the Netherlands rather than an acceptance of an alternative view of worthwhile knowledge.

Denmark

Danish 'community education' has been admired and copied in other countries since the end of the nineteenth century. Its context is a relatively egalitarian society in which community values have been powerful. The social unity of Denmark has been based historically upon one people, one language and one church (Lutheran). It is also founded traditionally on a population of small farmers living in village communities. The aristocratic landowning class was destroyed by the agricultural depression of the late nineteenth century, leaving behind co-operatives of newly independent farmers as the main form of rural organization. This distinctive rural, egalitarian, co-operative culture had an impact even on the urban and national identity, especially in historic attempts to resist German annexation. Even with rapid urbanization and the growth of manufacturing industry since 1945, which has left only 16 per cent of the population in the countryside, these traditional rural values have continued to have a major influence.

The traditional rural community identity has had an impact on the education system in four main ways. First, schooling is confined to mornings only so as not to remove children too much from the familial environment and, for similar reasons, compulsory schooling does not begin until the age of seven. Secondly, compulsory schooling from 7 to 16 is covered entirely within a single institution – the *folkeskole*. This school has a socially integrative, familial ethos so there is no streaming or setting before the last two grades and, as far as possible, the same teacher stays with a class as it progresses through the grades. Third, the Danish *folkeskole* is controlled by governing bodies dominated by parents in which teachers are only observers. These councils have considerable rights of consultation over, for instance, the appointment of teachers and the details of the curriculum.[53] Fourth, the Danish community school had its own philosopher and spokesman in N.F.S. Grundtvig (1783–1872) who provided it with a consistent and coherent rationale.

The importance of Grundtvig should not be underestimated. He shared with his compatriot and near contemporary Søren Kierkegaard a critical attitude to prevailing rationalism and system-building in the mid-nineteenth century and, also like Kierkegaard, Grundtvig's philosophy derived from Lutheran piety, a romantic folk nationalism and an austere empathy with the suffering of the Danish peasantry. Whereas Kierkegaard escaped into a subjective, existential philosophy which achieved universal recognition only in the mid-twentieth century, Grundtvig focused upon the richness and goodness of the rural community which he attempted to enhance through his literary work and especially the Folk High School. This institution was for young adults and aimed to develop both the folk culture and the processes of democratic decision.[54] Grundtvig was the most authentic European proponent of the transmission of individually liberating, socially cohesive and egalitarian 'community knowledge'. He anticipated later non-European schemes of John Dewey, Mahatma Gandhi and Paulo Freire.

The Folk High Schools survive but, as adult institutions, they are not central to Danish educational provision. They are a monument to Grundtvig's ideas, the real impact of which is reflected in the community orientation and egalitarianism of the *folkeskole*. So when secondary education was reorganized in Denmark in 1975, the differentiated systems of the Federal Republic of Germany and of the Netherlands were rejected, as was the split between primary and lower secondary schooling of most other European countries. One folk entailed one school. The *folkeskole* became a community-controlled school to a degree not matched elsewhere in Europe and its curriculum and organization deliberately set out to foster the intellectual freedom of the individual as well as the democratic decision-making of students which Grundtvig had encouraged.[55] Furthermore, and this dates from the nineteenth century, groups of parents were allowed to establish their own schools to reflect their own ideological identities which would be state financed but totally free from state control.[56]

Curriculum and curriculum change

There are limits to curriculum autonomy in the *folkeskole*. The national Ministry of Education determines the subjects of study and the broad objectives of each subject. However, these subjects are less encyclopaedic than in other European countries. Only Danish (including Norwegian and Swedish at some stages), mathematics, Christian studies and physical education are compulsory in every grade. Two foreign languages (English and German or French) must be provided by schools for students in upper grades. The other subjects which must be made available by schools are more community orientated – sex education, road safety, world religions, contemporary affairs, health education in relation to alcohol and drugs, and vocational guidance.[57] This curriculum is little different from the 'social problem' orientation of the American high school.

The national curriculum must be made available by schools but parents collectively can modify the suggested content and there is considerable emphasis, even for quite young children, on the prior negotiation of content between teachers and pupils. The same kind of choice applies in examinations. Up to 11 subjects may be taken in partly external examinations at the end of the eighth, ninth or (post-compulsory) tenth grades but students can opt to take any number of subjects in any combination. Informal teacher assessment prevails before this point and carries more weight than formal examinations in the eighth to tenth grades.[58]

The individualist and community orientation in Danish education is reduced in the latter grades of the *folkeskole*. It comes to an abrupt halt after the end of that course. Upper secondary academic education is as standardized and encyclopaedic as any in Europe. The *gymnasium* curriculum is controlled by the national Ministry of Education which determines the subjects of study, time allocations and, in detail, the topics to be covered in each subject. The *gymnasium* course culminates in the *studentereksamen* which gives entry to higher education. This is a state qualification which is awarded after national written and school-based oral examinations.

The *Gymnasium* curriculum in Denmark has the same language and mathematics focus of the classic encyclopaedic curriculum in other parts of Europe. There is a common core of Danish, religion, German and/or English, French or Russian, history, civics, classical civilization and mathematics as well as physical education, art and music. Students follow either the language line with core studies also in Latin, geography and biology or the mathematics line with core subjects of physics and chemistry. There are then specialized studies with separate orientations – Latin and Greek or modern languages or modern languages and social studies in the language line and physical sciences or biological sciences or science and social studies in the mathematics line.[59] This curriculum is universalist and it is founded on the linguistic/mathematical starting points which typify encyclopaedism elsewhere.

Upper secondary vocational education in Denmark has been more difficult to enter than the *gymnasium* because of limitation on the number of places. This form of preparation is closely linked to the *gymnasium* curriculum and gives entry to higher education. Vocational schooling is not a dumping ground for academic failures.

Danish universities, especially the oldest, in Copenhagen, have retained a German tradition of academic freedom, a humanist bias in studies and an equivalent of *Freiheit des Studiums* which means that students take up to eight years to complete a degree. However, also as in the Federal Republic, there are a variety of institutions of technical higher education which have helped to prevent universities dominating school education.

Denmark has achieved the institutional separation of distinct views of knowledge which seemed possible at one time in the German Federal Republic but which was subverted by the achievement ethos creeping down the school system. A 'community orientation' applies to the education and the knowledge diet of all children up to 16 to a degree that is not paralleled anywhere else in Europe. Yet the rational encyclopaedic tradition is just as powerfully entrenched in upper secondary schooling as in any other country of Western Europe. On top of this is a humanist tradition in universities which, like that of the German Federal Republic, has been prevented from infecting the school system. While Denmark's education system is not necessarily adapted to a European future of a high-technology economy and diverse nomadic society, it indicates, in ways that do not seem to be understood in France or England, that quite different values can apply to separate sectors of education without reducing coherence or social opportunity.

Conclusion

It was assumed at the beginning that German, Dutch and Danish approaches to school knowledge were quite different from those prevailing in southern Europe. The assumption largely holds in the Netherlands and Denmark where a community orientation at lower levels can co-exist happily with rational encyclopaedism in upper secondary education. The exception – and a very major one – is the German Federal Republic. Encyclopaedism is well established but the naturalist views, which are central to traditional German culture, seem to have been undermined, though not totally excluded, by the dominance of the achievement ethic.

The Federal Republic of Germany is so important in the European Community that its approaches are likely to have a major impact on European education as a whole. This educational future will not be healthy until the Federal Republic re-asserts its cultural authenticity and authority at home and abroad. European education may then draw as fully upon German naturalism as upon French rationalism.

Chapter Five
The Humanist Periphery

England and Wales, Ireland, and Greece are not only on the geographic periphery of Europe. Their failure to join in the mainstream of European educational rationalism threatens to make them economically and socially marginal in a single market Europe. In Greece and Ireland, humanist culture was established through a nationalism which preceded economic development. Economic change may yet modify a high culture without particularly deep roots.

In England and Wales humanism is associated with the pre-industrial values which survived and reasserted themselves after nineteenth-century industrialization. The depth of tradition means that radical change may be very difficult and painful. But the distinctive character of English humanism may permit it to seek different routes to rationality and individual choice.

England and Wales

England and Wales, unlike Scotland, give little weight in education to rational, methodical and systematic knowledge objectives. Rational intelligence is assumed to be an innate characteristic which does not need training in the intellectual élite and which is not worth developing in others. If that is the case then education in England and Wales may fail to provide the 'public' knowledge which is recognized in most other European countries as central to occupational success. The first question is, what is the place, if any, of rational knowledge in the school curriculum?

There is a second question. English education has been noted, historically, for a child-centred, individualist orientation. Can these traditional conceptions accommodate the private and community knowledge demands which, it has been suggested, may become more insistent in a single market Europe?

Rationality in modern English educational culture

Foreign observers claim that English schooling gives little emphasis to the development of rational thought because English culture is anti-rational. The English are perceived as regarding thought as the enemy of action and as judging intellectual speculation as frivolous.[1] They are 'gifted with a vigorous defensive instinct against all unhealthy intellectual curiosity.'[2] Theory is differentiated from practice and is viewed as the distinctly subordinate partner.

This leaves the English incapable of negotiating a world of sophisticated economic, social and political organization where the success of action depends on its location in elaborated chains of schematic connection. To assume that English culture is constitutionally anti-rational is to accept that its people have no occupational futures except as poets and peasants.

The hostility to rationalism in English culture is also a pose and an affectation. Historical culture in England is studded with great rational system-builders including Newton, Hobbes, and Darwin.[3] At the apex of education and scholarship in the twentieth century, substantial and original work has been done in physics, chemistry and anthropology which have involved major intellectual system-building. In history, literature, philosophy and most branches of social and political science, dominant approaches have been empirical and there has been a hostility to theoretical or speculative intellectual architecture . Star-gazing in itself is not held to be illegitimate. Rather there is a suspicion that it will lead to neglect of the ground on which the astronomer is standing.

Rationality has had an obscured place in traditional élite education in England. Classicists may have concentrated upon the humane, heroic and aesthetic insights that the study of Greek and Latin philosophy, literature and history might yield, but their studies were based on a thorough mastery of the rational structures of the languages. Similar conditions applied to modern foreign language study. Physicists, chemists and biologists needed mathematics in much the same way. Of all the British universities in the period of expansion from the mid-1960s, it was Oxford and Cambridge which, almost alone, continued to insist that all entrants should have competence in the logical studies of mathematics or a science and two foreign languages.

Rational capacity in English élite education has been seen as a precondition of study rather than as a desired outcome. It became the covert means of identifying a future élite who could benefit from the highest levels of education. Once selected, the 'intelligent' (i.e. those with innate rational capacities) were given a humanist education which aimed at the development of moral and aesthetic 'feeling'. But those deemed to lack this rational capacity were condemned to lower-status education. A major weakness of English schooling since 1945 has been that democratized education has aimed at the outward badges of culture such as humanist sensitivity. The Masonic handshake of élite status has been rational intelligence which has not been challenged in attempts to widen social opportunities through education.

Individualism and community

English educationists have traditionally prided themselves on the encouragement and respect that schools give to the individuality of pupils and their wider social, moral and emotional personalities. These virtues have pertained not only to 'progressive' primary schools. They have been as much part of the historical culture of élite secondary schools and universities. There has been less success in linking educational knowledge to communities in the wider world. Schools may be often harmonious and creative collectivities of children and youth. But this has been achieved by erecting barriers against the world outside.

'Individualism' and a concern for the 'whole child' are sufficiently deep rooted for these values to survive pressures for a standardized curriculum and, indeed, for a stronger place for training in rationality. It is not only general educational culture but also the roles of teachers and the ways that they regard themselves which give continued vitality to English individualism.

This individualism is not an unmitigated good. Darker forces of class distinction lie behind it and emerge in its application. These can be expressed in stereotyping. Social class attitudes have conditioned perceptions about appropriate education for groups or 'types' of children over the entire history of public education. The British are aware of it. Foreigners observing English education perceive it even more strikingly. But perceptions alone do not change attitudes and behaviours.

Stereotyping in this sense involves classifying individual children as one of a group or type with fixed characteristics and treating him or her educationally according to the stereotype. It has had a long history in England. In the late nineteenth century, social class was overtly and unashamedly suggested as the basis for educational differentiation.[4] In the twentieth century there have been Norwood's aptitudes – academic, technical and practical – upon which different kinds of secondary education could be based. There has been the subsequent labelling by language use, by race and ethnic origin and by sex. English individualism can very easily lapse into pigeon-holing which is antithetical to personal choice and autonomy.

Individualism in English education has also tended to operate on the basis of teachers' perceptions of individual needs and wishes. Families and wider communities have not participated in the definitions. English education has had a particular blind spot towards community values and knowledge. The primordial community has been that of pupils and teachers, whether in the élite private boarding school or in urban state primary education. They are moral and social communities which supplant the family rather than complement it. Indeed there has been a tradition of hostility between parents and school-teachers dating from the time of the introduction of compulsory schooling in the large cities in the nineteenth century, which was mirrored by the scarcely less veiled moral or social contempt of the reformed 'public' schools towards the families of many of their pupils.

Other kinds of communities have had little impact. English state schools since 1902 have been administered by Local Authorities which have been too large to represent any cohesive communities. Links with work and with employers have been regarded with suspicion by teachers who argue that schools aim to provide a broader vision than that of occupational futures. The religious groups which have been recognized historically have been those Christian denominations which have had their own schools. Their distinctiveness has been effectively usurped by state funding. Of the minority languages only Welsh has been provided for systematically. More recent immigrant cultural minorities have struggled against a conception of the school as a multicultural institution which has the function of integrating children from different cultures in a school community defined exclusively by teachers.

How far have changes in the provision and organization of schooling since the provision of universal secondary education after 1944 encouraged or obstructed the adoption of curricula which make better provision for the acquisition of both rational 'public' knowledge and that appropriate for individuals in wider communities?

Changing schools and changing curriculum

The most significant change in schooling in England and Wales has been the introduction of comprehensive secondary schools, largely in the 1960s and 1970s. This change has been also one of the major influences on primary education. In both primary and secondary education, the school reorganization of the 1960s led initially to greater powers for teachers in curriculum construction at school level.

However, the direction which curriculum change took after the mid-1960s in both primary and secondary schools has been abruptly affected by the enactment of a scheme for a national curriculum in 1988. While a similar pattern of curriculum change towards teacher- and school-level decision-making in the late 1960s and early 1970s, and then a return to more rigid external definition in the 1980s, can be detected in other countries such as Spain, France and the German Federal Republic, it promises to be so dramatic in England and Wales that the process of curriculum change needs to be considered in two phases – before and after the 1988 Education Reform Act.

Primary schools

The 'child-centred English primary school curriculum' is a phrase that has been repeated so often inside and outside Britain that the number of serious questions it begs are easily forgotten. Official support for a child-centred approach has been undoubted from the early years of the twentieth century. Many primary school teachers were trained in institutions of teacher education in which they were encouraged to adopt 'progressive' methods. They were subsequently urged, even cajoled, into maintaining this ethos by official reports and by inspectors/advisers. Many had a deep commitment to a pedagogy which allowed children to engage in creative activities, to discover actively rather than absorb passively, to pursue individual interests and to develop skills and knowledge relevant to a range of conventional subjects through practical, often locally focused and co-operative projects.

Many schools and teachers went only partly down this road and adopted working styles which were not very different from those advocated in France in the late 1970s – that is, specified hours, topics and attainment targets for language and computation and more flexible, interdisciplinary, child-centred approaches in other areas. As long as the 11-plus examination, with its standard written papers in English and arithmetic (as well as that testing 'intelligence') continued to prevail, which in most authorities meant the early 1960s, this dual approach was the furthest that most schools could move towards an individualist curriculum.[5]

A full-blown 'child-centred' curriculum was only a realistic possibility in most English primary schools for a period of little more than 20 years and it is unlikely that many schools were able to do much for very long between the weaning of one generation of teachers from 11-plus cramming and the self-protective reactions of the next to the growing attacks on the neglect of central areas of the curriculum from the mid-1970s which culminated in the 1988 Education Reform Act.

Yet it may be unfair to accuse the child-centred movement in primary schooling of undermining the capacity of English primary schools to provide a grounding in pre-rational knowledge, especially in areas such as language and computation. If English primary schools are deficient in this respect – and there is little comparative evidence to support it –[6] then at most the child-centred curriculum provided the circumstances in which this inadequacy could persist.

Neglect or inefficient teaching of language and mathematics as well as of modern foreign languages and science in primary schools can be related to deficiencies of secondary education. Fully qualified primary school teachers have been incompetent in areas such as mathematics, sciences, modern languages and, less frequently, mother tongue, because the structure of the secondary and higher education curriculum has not required them to be proficient in these subjects.[7]

All children have progressed conventionally through the grades of primary education without repeating years because of long-held conceptions of chronologically-defined communities of children. The exclusion of parents from school matters meant that there was relatively little consumer pressure on teachers to raise standards or expectations. The mentality of a society rigidly divided on social class lines has meant that even primary school teachers can accept easily that large numbers of children will be educational failures. The values of the nineteenth century 'Board Schools', which in the large cities had the physical appearance as well as the concomitant attitudes of citadels of an alien army of occupation, have not completely disappeared. These values as much determine what happens in primary schools as the predominant views of worthwhile knowledge.

The introduction of the national curriculum from 1989 may not be as significant a force as has been supposed in helping all children to acquire the capacity for rational and systematic thought and action. The core subjects of mother tongue and mathematics are conventional, and only science may be an innovation in many schools. The foundation areas are also those traditionally taught such as history, geography, music, art and physical education as well as the newer area of technology. But this curriculum, without specified hours, still allows a flexibility through which the broad approaches of the past can be maintained.

It is unlikely that primary school teachers brought up on a child-centred philosophy, and having the advantage not possessed by most of their counterparts in other European countries of formal equality of grades and status with secondary school teachers, will abandon 'progressive' approaches lightly. There is little reason why they should. Discovery methods, individual learning and opportunities for creativity can continue within new curriculum frameworks. Even with these sanctions, there is little that can be done to stop determined and committed teachers from employing the pedagogy they believe to be right, as historical examples in France and Italy indicate. Even in the most authoritarian education systems there are aspects of the curriculum and the organization of schools in which what happens behind closed, or even partly open, classroom doors is a private matter between a teacher and his or her own pupils.

Changes in assessment and parent rights contained in the 1988 Act and the legislation/regulations which preceded it are perhaps more significant. The 1988 Act appears to foreshadow an external control of teaching through assessment which is not matched in any other European Community country. In the German Federal Republic, it has been seen, assessment of attainment of primary school children can be extremely thorough, meticulous and overly fastidious. But it can be also more relaxed in some *Länder*. Everywhere in the Republic, however, it is a matter for teachers individually or collectively at school level. Elsewhere in Europe teachers are trusted to assess even where they are required legally or contractually to assess, and where their judgements can be challenged externally. Whether external assessment at 11 (assuming external examination will not occur at 7) will produce higher general standards of attainment in the core, pre-rational subjects is difficult to speculate upon since there are no comparative examples upon which to draw.

The position of parents is more important. The 1988 Act in effect makes parents the watchdogs of standards of attainment since they alone have effective power of action where standards are not met. However, this is power of a different kind from that found in most European countries, where class as well as school councils allow parents more direct and continuous contact with teachers than is proposed in England. Parent power in England will be distant yet absolute, through freedom of choice of schools for their children. Parents will have opportunities to punish ineffective schools and teachers rather than to participate in negotiations with them or even to encourage them. There is a question of whether the market-forces approach to parental power will lead to higher standards of attainment in core subjects or whether parents will be sufficiently active in these conditions to bring a range of pressures on teachers.

Secondary schooling

Despite political perceptions that the weaknesses of the school curriculum in England and Wales apply to the whole period of compulsory schooling from ages 5 to 16, the major problems have been concentrated largely on the secondary level, from ages 11 to 18. The questions about the capacity of schools to provide rational, systematic and universal knowledge for most pupils and to react to individual and community knowledge demands can be examined in relation to three historical phases. There was the period from 1944 when a full system of state secondary education developed but of a differentiated kind. This was followed by the period roughly since the mid-1960s when attempts were made to create a common curriculum for comprehensive schools. Finally there are the implications of the 1988 national curriculum proposals.

There was never any equivalent in England and Wales to the French *lycée* or the German *Gymnasium* – that is state schools directly controlled by central government from the early nineteenth century. Instead there were private grammar schools of varying status which had existed in many cases from the sixteenth century or before. In the mid-nineteenth century, a number broke away from the pack and became boarding schools (in London also some day schools) for the upper and upper middle classes ('public' schools). Other high status day schools retained a loose link with government through funding ('Direct Grant Schools') until they also became largely private schools rather than become comprehensive from the late 1970s. The remainder were absorbed gradually into the state education system from 1870 by taking their new entrants from state primary schools in return for local authority financial support.

The independent 'public' schools, though taking only 7 per cent of all school-age children in the 1980s, dominated the character of English secondary education until the 1960s and beyond. The humanist values of the public school curriculum were accepted largely by many local authority grammar schools, especially as they aimed to prepare students for university entrance. The humanist philosophy was reflected in the high status of classics and later arts subjects and in the actual content of subjects such as history, English and foreign literature.

Central government, through the Board of Education, issued a national curriculum of prescribed subjects (though without time allocations) from 1904 to 1922.[8] Perhaps more important was the structure of the School Certificate and the entrance requirements of the universities which controlled these examinations. Candidates were required to reach prescribed standards in five subjects which included English, mathematics or a science and a foreign language. A common curriculum prevailed and all students were expected to cover the core subjects.

Two developments undermined this early-twentieth-century encyclo-paedism. First, universities began to demand passes in the Higher School Certificate which focused on three, usually cognate, subjects taken over a period of two years by students aged 16–18.[9] The specialized 'sixth' form curriculum, which had existed in the prestigious public schools in the later nineteenth century, had become obligatory for all university entrants by 1945. Universalism was breached.

Second, the School Certificate was replaced by the General Certificate of Education (GCE) in 1951 which, in effect, permitted students to specialize from the age of 14. Passes were awarded in any number of individual subjects. The core of English, mathematics or science and a foreign language was destroyed. Universities still required five subjects for entry but at least two were to be at 'Advanced' level which replaced the Higher School Certificate. In practice, students expected to aim at higher education were encouraged to take only those subjects required for entrance. Weaker pupils were allowed to concentrate on those subjects in which they had a reasonable chance of success.

Comprehensive schools grew especially after a government circular of 1965 and replaced the grammar schools together with the low-status secondary modern schools which had been set up after 1944. Compre-hensive schools reinforced the tendency towards low expectations for below-average pupils. The grammar school curriculum survived for the quarter of the comprehensive school intake which previously had been selected for grammar schools since the GCE also survived. Around 40 per cent took a watered-down version of the GCE, the Certificate of Secondary Education (CSE). When these two examinations were amalgamated in 1986, the new General Certificate of Secondary Education (GCSE) continued to allow candidates to be awarded certificates for any number of subjects with no obligation to pass any specific subjects. Even the national curriculum from 1989 onwards which will require schools to provide teaching in the same core and foundation subjects as primary schools (with the addition of a modern foreign language) will not require students to pass any particular subjects to gain certificates. Students in practice will still be able to neglect the core areas of rational knowledge. (10)

Though comprehensive schools mainly cater for the 11–18 age group (with two cycle variants), the upper secondary curriculum for 16–18-year-olds has been relatively unaffected by secondary school reorgani- • zation. This level has no common curriculum. Students still specialize exclusively in any three subjects of their choice which the school can provide. There is no obligation to take any of the core subjects of the national curriculum. It is rare to find upper secondary school students in England who study more than two of English, mathematics, a science subject and a modern language. Many students will take none of these. Attempts to widen the 'sixth form' curriculum have met so far with little success. Even the practice, introduced in the 1980s, of allowing students to take more subjects with a lighter content ('AS' levels) has few takers and does not demand any compulsory areas of study.

Upper secondary schooling, in practice, is restricted mainly to the very small numbers of students who enter higher education.[11] As a result only 46 per cent of 16-year-olds were in school in 1985 and fewer than 20 per cent completed Advanced level GCE courses. This restriction is worsened by the nature of opportunities for technical and vocational education at upper secondary level. These courses focus on occupational areas and have relatively restricted general education elements compared to equivalent courses in other European countries.

Despite the clamour in Britain, the national curriculum scheme of 1988 is a half-hearted attempt to meet problems of neglect of central areas of school knowledge at secondary education level. Students will have to study a common curriculum up to the age of 16 and will be assessed in each element of it. Beyond the age of 16, students will continue to be positively discouraged from following a broad curriculum or even all the core, rational subjects. As a consequence, half the entrants to higher education at the age of 18 will continue to be barely numerate, the other half will have limited literary capacities and the majority will have studied no foreign language from the age of 16.

The national curriculum goes only part way to giving most students access to the range of subjects which may encourage rational, logical and systematic thought, communication and action. There is no immediate prospect of the situation in France or the German Federal Republic applying, where all 17–18-year-olds study mother tongue, a foreign language and mathematics and must reach minimum standards of attainment in each of these areas if they are to gain recognized qualifications. English students will still be deprived of the kind of access to universal knowledge which their equivalents elsewhere have had as a matter of course.

However, the failings of the English curriculum are as much evident in the objectives and content of individual subjects as in the spread of subjects in the overall curriculum. The anti-rationalism of the conventionally rational subjects should be considered a little more fully.

Anti-rationalism in the content of secondary school subjects

The humanist approach of élite education was largely adopted to underwrite the curriculum of the comprehensive secondary schools of the 1960s. The argument was understandable. If comprehensive schools were to provide equality of opportunity then they should give common access to the élite curriculum. That such a curriculum was based on a view of knowledge which was anachronistic even for the existing élite was hardly considered.

So the objectives of teaching literature and history to a mass secondary school clientele were little different from those which had applied in the nineteenth-century public schools. The objectives of encouraging moral insight, appreciation of heroic human achievement and aesthetic sensibility changed little. One example may illustrate this development. The Schools Council Humanities Project of the late 1960s was aimed at a mass secondary school population. Traditional subject boundaries were dissolved through the focus on topics such as war and peace, poverty and the family. The pedagogy emphasized pupil discussion managed by a 'neutral' teacher/chairperson. The material was diverse and visual as well as literary. But the material was largely of a 'heroic' kind and dominated the whole pedagogic procedure. The clear aim was to develop moral sensitivity through exposure to fine texts. The project's director, Lawrence Stenhouse, argued that 'fine texts' should be the basis of mass secondary education because they could be appreciated intuitively by all levels of pupil.[12]

The weakness of the humanist view was that it was intrinsically élitist and appropriate to a pre-industrial society. The consequences of the adoption of this position in comprehensive schools were also to deny a purpose and status to rational and systematic study. Even in the teaching of English battle positions were drawn up over the place of grammar, which one side regarded as a pollutant of creativity and the other as the basis of rigour – arguments which would have been seen as arcane even in the 'rational' approach to language teaching of the late nineteenth-century French *lycée*. The study of history for democratic humanists concentrated on empathy with the poor and oppressed and for traditionalists on the heroism of British political history. The most that could be offered in terms of method and system was an emphasis on 'objective' consideration of sources by the progressives and a stress on chronology by the traditionalists.

However, it was subjects such as mathematics, the sciences and foreign languages which were beached without a convincing purpose or rationale. Projects in mathematics and science which were introduced in the 1960s emphasized practical observation and discovery.[13] Justifications were sought in child-centred discovery methods, though the approaches conveniently coincided with English tastes for empirical investigation. Despite the claims for novelty, these projects often reinforced the traditional English approach of making children work through endless and meaningless examples, with little concern for formal learning of principles, a method which had been criticized at the end of the nineteenth century.[14] The assumption that children would grasp general principles as a result of active discovery only began to be challenged in the late 1980s.[15]

These fundamental problems of the conception of worthwhile knowledge are not touched by the national curriculum. Those guidelines which have so far appeared on mathematics and science define objectives only in terms of a content of certain precise rules (and often simply information) that should be mastered.[16] There is no feeling in any of the statements that the mathematics and science curricula should prepare pupils to think and act rationally and systematically in a high-technology economy. The 'rational' subjects still lack an epistemological purpose. They are vaguely thought to be useful. There is little concept that they are worth learning in themselves because they might provide fruitful ways for students to participate with confidence in a rationally structured human universe.[17]

Private knowledge and private cultures and the English secondary school
Secondary schools suffer from the same self-imposed isolation from wider communities as has been discussed in relation to primary education. Three conditions make the situation worse in secondary schools. First, there are the strong subject orientations of traditional English secondary schools which divide schools internally (and militate against even an integrated school-based community of children) and which discourage attempts to relate learning to the locality – as has been found in primary schools. Second, there are the latent valuations of teachers and members of society generally about class-divisions which make it easy to reject pupils as inevitable failures. This process has been

identified particularly in secondary schools and has been the subject of a considerable literature which, however, does not always identify it as part of an especially English disease. Third, the humanist view of worthwhile knowledge is based on a 'high culture' which does not even make the pretence to any universal and democratic relevance. As a result English secondary schooling has not only alienated youth cultures (since similar phenomena are found elsewhere) but it is also alienated from popular and class cultures to a degree not experienced in, say, Denmark or the German Federal Republic.

This cultural isolation of English schools applies also to preparation for work. Much of the criticism of secondary schools since the mid-1970s has focused on the anti-industrial attitudes which they are claimed to encourage.[18] The 1983 Technical and Vocational Education Initiative (TVEI) was a response which was designed to facilitate the transition from school to work in ways similar to the German *Arbeitslehre*. But work-cultures in Britain have never had close contacts with formal education as in the German Federal Republic. School teachers believe that schooling provides something higher than the alienating world of employment. This is understandable when trade unions and employers have often shared this concept of work. 'Vocations' have been limited to certain occupations which unusually offer personal satisfaction. But these work cultures have been firmly separated from formal education.

It is doubtful that TVEI has had any significant effect on moral and social attitudes to work. Instead, it has developed in much the same way as in other Western European countries with an emphasis on 'generic skills' which sometimes does mean training in systematic thought and action. Work-related education in English schooling may actually become a rationalist Trojan horse in an anti-rational school culture.

Humanism, rationality and the limits of English educational culture
The prospects for English education and thus for the English and Welsh people in an integrated Europe (or even in a high-technology world economy) which this analysis has suggested are rather depressing. Despite a curriculum reform of 1988 which has been seen to be far-reaching and dramatic, there is little evidence that English schools, teachers and educational authorities want the majority of pupils to be taught to think and act in the systematic and rational way which their equivalents in the other major European countries believe is essential for survival in the world of the future.

Sir Michael Sadler, when faced with a similarly depressing conclusion almost a century ago, sought consolation in the idea that formal education never really mattered as much in England as in France or Germany and that the English believed, with some justification, that real education began after schooling was finished (see above p. 73). Perhaps this is the ultimate solace. English education can remain an esoteric and self-contained culture which isolates children and youth from the rest of life on the assumption that they can be reborn as complete human beings at the age of 16, 18 or 21. The resilience of English culture is indicated by the relative success of this scheme up to the present.

The difficulty is that, in an economically unified Europe, English school leavers will be distinctly backward compared to their European peers when they enter the labour market, unless they compete in areas where only unsystematic creativity and consistently moral behaviour count. But even this assumes that English education works by its own standards. The alienation of large sections of the population (including many students) from schooling means that the purposes of knowledge transmission will not be met. There is little evidence that English schooling can become any more responsive to popular cultures than education in France or the German Federal Republic, or that it will be able to meet the choices of active participants as opposed to passive consumers as well as some of the other European countries.

Other cases of a surviving humanist tradition

The survival of a humanist curriculum in Greece and Ireland is widely perceived to be an obstacle to 'modernization'. The basis of this humanism is different from that in England. In Greece, conceptions of a national culture based on a Hellenic tradition and the power of the Greek Orthodox religion have supported a school curriculum which is inordinately biased towards literary-humane studies. In Ireland, humanistic education is a survival of historical British colonialism but is also supported by a cultural conservatism to which the Catholic church has contributed. In both these countries, there has been a relatively centralized control of the curriculum and a 'common' core of studies which has been missing in England and Wales. In neither does the English 'action-orientation' of humanism have much importance.

Greece

The major socio-political issue for over a century has been Greek national identity. Independence from the Ottoman Empire from the 1820s left Greece without a powerful pre-existing social and political élite. The emerging professional, commercial and political classes sought a Hellenic authenticity derived from classical Greece as well as from Greek Orthodox Christianity.

One outcome was the development of an artificial 'high culture' language – *katharevousa* – which contained elements of classical and Byzantine Greek and became the language of government and administration. The majority of the population used the popular *demotike*. The language issue has been central in educational policy debates especially since the 1950s, until *demotike* effectively triumphed from the late 1970s.[19] More deeply rooted has been the moral-revelatory core of Greek Orthodox epistemology which contrasts with the power of Jesuitical rationalism in western Catholicism.

Though parliamentary monarchy existed in the nineteenth century it was not until after 1949, following German occupation and then civil war, that a more democratic and progressive government became possible. This process was interrupted by a dictatorship from 1967–74. Reform of education together with recognition of popular aspirations and attempts to modernize the economy were foreshadowed in the period from 1957 to 1965 but only began to be implemented after 1974. In this respect there are parallels between Greece and Spain and Portugal.

Education has been undeveloped in Greece as in these other countries. Despite laws as early as 1834, schooling did not become compulsory in practice until after 1929, and then only for the age group 6–11. Secondary education for all, in common lower secondary schools, was introduced from 1977 as the period of compulsory education was extended from six to nine years. This change inevitably meant a reconsideration of the purpose and content of the traditionally humanist and selective secondary school system.

Greek educational humanism

The humanist tradition in modern Greek education has been supported by its political position in the historical nationalist movement. It has been undermined almost to the point of sterility by its lack of a powerful epistemological and educational rationale. The curriculum of élite education is heavily orientated towards the study of ancient Greece but in order to give emphasis to a special Greek collective identity rather than to produce a distinctive kind of individual morality and sensitivity.

The central position of the study of classical Greece in the curriculum emerged from the attempt to create a national identity in the nineteenth and early twentieth centuries after centuries of Ottoman domination.

Yet there was always an arrogant and megalomaniac streak in this nationalism: 'If the modern Greeks had not even had this deficient knowledge of Ancient Greek, they would have turned into one more Balkan race.'[20] A similar view was taken towards the international Greek Orthodox church. This version of Greek nationalism began to be associated with conservative political groupings and was viewed increasingly with suspicion by the political left and centre especially after the junta government of the dictatorship of 1967–74 tried to use a Hellenic-Greek Orthodox ideology to underwrite its rule. So political parties on the left and centre attempted to restrict the place in education of both *katharevousa* and of ancient Greece.

In educational politics, however, classical humanism has been more strongly supported. The School of Philosophy of the University of Athens (where languages, literature and history are taught as well as philosophy) has been the centre for the preservation of the humanist tradition. It has maintained links with the secondary school teachers' union, whose members have been trained largely in this University School.[21]

There is also a wider consumer support for humanist education. The School of Philosophy at Athens retains the highest prestige. The proportion of students in universities following courses in the humanities is one of the highest in Europe. Indeed for a long period science and medical education was very undeveloped in higher education. Social values of aspiring to professional status focus particularly on those occupations requiring a humanistic educational background.

Changing school and changing curriculum
The 1976 Educational Reform was supported by all political parties in reaction to the extreme cultural and educational conservatism of the deposed junta. As well as extending compulsory schooling to nine years and creating a common lower secondary school (*gymnasium*), the reform made some attempt to change the curriculum by extending upper secondary level vocational education, introducing *demotike* as the medium of secondary education and replacing some classical Greek texts by modern Greek translations.

Yet the aims of this law still reflected a political/national humanism. The new comprehensive *Gymnasium* was to

> help (pupils) to become conscious of their abilities and inclinations; to sharpen their moral judgement; to develop their religious and national conscience.[22]

There is little in the law which suggests that developing a rational or scientific type of thinking has any special importance.

School curriculum content reveals the persisting humanist view. The primary schooling is conventional – religion, Greek, history, geography, study of the environment, arts and crafts, arithmetic, science, music and civics. A similar core curriculum applies at both levels of secondary education but the time allocations are heavily biased towards Greek, with classical Greek literature (increasingly in modern Greek translation) having more teaching time than any other subject even in the *Gymnasium*. In the upper secondary *lyceum* the bias towards humanities is even stronger, with even more hours for classical Greek as well as Latin.[23] In the final two grades of the *lyceum* there is a distinction between humanities and science options, but even students of the latter spend almost 60 per cent of their time on classical studies.[24]

This humanist curriculum is national and compulsory. There are standard numbers of hours, content and textbooks dictated by the national Ministry of Education for all levels of schooling, modified only by limited choices in the final grades of upper secondary schooling and by the different curricula of the technical *lyceum* which was introduced by the 1976 Law. The association of humanism with individualism and specialization that emerged in England never had any place in Greek schools.

Indeed there is a a mechanical approach which is associated with sterile encyclopaedism elsewhere. The criticisms noted by the OECD (Organization of Economic Co-operation and Development) examiners in 1982 were that the curriculum was overloaded. There was too much factual rote learning and too much formal instruction. There was little opportunity for class discussion or independent work.[25] These criticisms are not unusual in any school system at its worst. But they would rarely apply *in toto* in a school system devoted to the individualist humanism of England.

The defeat of a humanist tradition in Greek education may depend on political rather than educational action. For it is in political-social attitudes that a humanist view is entrenched. It may be a formalist and sterile view of a literary legacy. But this formalism is based upon conceptions of a national culture and of the characteristics of an élite which are not easily changed simply within the school system.

Ireland

The Irish humanist tradition is as much a product of historical British colonialism as the educational approaches found in former British colonies outside Europe. Yet, like some of these other countries, an independent Ireland after 1922 drew upon indigenous traditions to achieve a national cultural authenticity which, ironically, reinforced the humanist dominance in school knowledge. Since the 1960s, government policy has been to widen educational opportunities and to provide the technical studies necessary for industrialization. But the humanist tradition has not been effectively confronted.

State primary schools were established under central control from 1831 – before, and in anticipation of, the introduction of state schooling in England.[26] These schools were secular/Protestant in an overwhelmingly Catholic country and used English exclusively when Irish Gaelic was still the language of a substantial proportion of the population. The curriculum throughout the nineteenth century mirrored practice in England (except for the greater degree of central control in Ireland). Secondary schools were modelled on English grammar schools except that they had more government support. They were exclusively Protestant. Alongside this colonial provision was an extensive informal system of 'hedge schools' which had the tacit approval of the Catholic church and which met with repression or neglect by the colonial authorities.

After Irish independence in 1922, policy was to introduce an Irish cultural perspective throughout the curriculum. In secondary schools, Irish was to be the medium and or a central subject in curriculum. History, geography and literature were to focus on the Irish experience.[27] This Irish culture was derived from both a historical popular culture and from Catholicism. Popular culture had developed over more than a thousand years and was expressed in epic and heroic poetry and romance.[28] The Catholic church after 1922 in effect gained control of many state schools (with over a third of enrolments) and adopted a conservative humanist approach to school knowledge. Political independence reinforced humanism to the extent that an official commission in 1960 could declare that the secondary school curriculum was and should be 'humanist and intellectual in character'.[29]

Changing school and changing curriculum
Recent educational reform dates from 1966 when the *Investment in Education* report, inspired by the OECD, urged school expansion and a greater attention to technical/vocational education.[30] Barriers to entry to secondary education were dropped, comprehensive and community secondary schools were established to challenge (but not replace) the older secondary schools and, in 1972, the period of compulsory

schooling was extended to the age of 15, which meant universal lower secondary schooling.

Unlike England, a national curriculum of subjects and content has always been prescribed in Irish schools. In practice it has been applied in a permissive way in primary schools since 1971 when a report was adopted which urged an individual and integrated approach to the primary curriculum rather similar to that of the Plowden Committee of 1967 in England.

In secondary schools there has been more rigid control especially through government dictation of compulsory subjects in the national examinations leading to the Intermediate Certificate (for 15-year-olds) and the Leaving Certificate (for 17-year-olds). Both examinations are based on a standard prescribed curriculum and require passes in six subjects for the Intermediate Certificate and in five for the Leaving Certificate.

This compulsory core curriculum has a humanist bias. The prescribed subjects for the Intermediate Certificate are Irish, English, mathematics and history/geography.[31] For the Leaving Certificate, students are advised to choose three of the minimum of five subjects from one area such as languages, science, business studies, social studies and applied science. But Irish is a compulsory subject and the universities usually specify that all students must have passes in Irish, English and a modern language. As a result, the number of students specializing in mathematics and sciences is very low.[32]

To move more towards the mainstream of European views of school knowledge, Ireland needs both to confront its own conception of a national culture inherited from the nineteenth-century nationalist movement and to challenge the English colonial and neo-colonial influences. In the 1970s it was perhaps more successful in doing the former than the latter.

Appendix: Scotland and Northern Ireland

Britain has a federal system of education. Two of the satellite members of the federation – Scotland and Northern Ireland – deserve special mention because views of school knowledge in these areas do differ from those of England and Wales.

Scotland is important particularly because an encyclopaedic tradition has prevailed which is closer to that of France or Germany than to that of England. Commonly it is associated with the lack of specialization in Scottish upper secondary and higher education compared to England – the Scottish Higher School Certificate examination is taken in five or six subjects compared to three 'A' levels in England and Scottish universities have a tradition of broad, multi-subject courses.

There is also a strong rational tradition in Scottish education which is marked by the logical and disputative style of analysis. The four Scottish universities of the eighteenth century focused on moral and natural philosophy which allowed for much stronger studies of pure science, medicine and economics than was found in England. Adam Smith's *Wealth of Nations* was based on a university lecture course. In the nineteenth century and into the twentieth century, university students would follow combinations which could span philosophy, languages, mathematics and science. The utilitarian outcomes of this approach were seen in the large number of Scottish university educated medical practitioners and engineers who worked in England and the British Empire.

Scottish distinctiveness has been undermined in the later twentieth century. Greater specialization has crept into universities. More significantly, the intellectual and educational vitality of Scotland, which has been claimed to produce an education system superior to that of England, has been eroded. The mass education system established following John Knox's *Book of Discipline* in the late sixteenth century, which led to higher proportions of poor children getting elementary, secondary and higher education even in the late nineteenth century than in England, has lost its advantages in the twentieth century. The values of English individualism have been less thoroughly accepted in Scotland but the weaknesses of a specialized and élitist education have not been prevented from crossing the border.

Contemporary hopes that membership of the European Community may reinvigorate Scottish culture and society may have some substance in that Scottish traditions may be more aligned to the rationalism which may be dominant in pan-European education. On the other hand there is a standardizing ethos in Scottish education which derives from its sixteenth-century Calvinist origins but which has also been reinforced by a relatively centralist approach to administration of the Scottish Office. Scottish education may be less receptive to demands for diversity. Its traditional function of encouraging emigration of the well-educated may be reinforced by the harmonizing impetus of an integrated Europe.[33]

In contrast, education in Northern Ireland, while administratively and legislatively separate, is closer in content and philosophy to that of England. The main difference is that state schools are patronized largely by Protestants while the Catholic schools have placed greater emphasis on Irish rather than British culture. But the curriculum is generally humanist in both kinds of school which have participated in the same GCE/GCSE examination system as in England.[34]

Chapter Six
Conclusion: What can be done?

European comparisons: limitations and opportunities

This review of the school curriculum in 12 nation states has focused on attitudes and intentions rather than practices and outcomes. It has tended to force infinite variety into fixed patterns. It does not provide firm evidence of the superiority of some national systems of education over others. The assessment of the relative strengths of education in the different countries is limited to the consonance of the aims of knowledge transmission with independent propositions of the future needs of children and young people. The propositions may be wrong and the evaluation thus rendered nugatory. Even if the propositions are valid their attainment may vary unequally from intentions in the different countries.

These points may be explored further. The broad views of what constitutes worthwhile knowledge, and the variations noted in their interpretation in different cultures and epochs, characterize the ways in which school knowledge is valued by educationists. Responses to these views are revealed in wide policy statements, in more precise curriculum plans, in the commentaries of those outside the final policy formulation process and in reports of typical practice. These views may be shared widely by other groups in society. They are internalized by teachers and others responsible for day-to-day pedagogic practice. It is reasonable to assume that what happens in classrooms broadly will mirror these dominant views. Yet it remains an assumption. Examples offered in this work were drawn more from curriculum objectives than from accounts of practice.

How could practice differ from intentions? Three points may be made. First, teachers may subscribe, perhaps without acknowledgement, to other views of knowledge than those assumed to prevail in

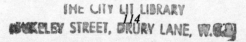

their teaching. Many teachers in England and Wales probably have pursued the encyclopaedic aims of universality and rationality within a broadly humanist framework. It is possible, for instance, to teach history in a way which covers other major branches of knowledge and which emphasizes systematic and logical thought. The 'hidden curriculum' of French schools may be humanist, as Bourdieu claims. In every time and place, teachers pursue naturalist or child-centred approaches, even unconsciously, when they behave as parents, members of tight-knit communities or as spontaneous human beings who temporarily set aside their formal pedagogic roles.

The broad traditions of knowledge should be seen as models against which a complex reality can be set heuristically rather than as definitive descriptions of this reality. Their value is as a tool for making sense of complexity. The limitations of such tools are that they yield little more than provisional and approximate insights.

Second, there can be good and bad teaching within each tradition. Only parenthetical references have been made in this book to the quality of teaching and learning by conventional criteria. Reference has been made to the downside of encyclopaedism. Too often, training in rationality degenerates into parrot learning, excessive intellectualism, student passivity in the face of an external and fixed body of knowledge or artificial party-games. Similar horror stories could be told about teaching in humanist or naturalist traditions. Examples in this work have been drawn more from high ideals rather than worst exemplars. Yet the potentialities of a view of knowledge may be judged as much by its weakest expositions as by its strongest.

Third, the preceding chapters have paid little attention to the conventional parameters of the quality issue. The resources of education which affect actual practice are susceptible to comparative European investigation – particularly the commitment of teachers, the effectiveness of schools as organizations and the socio-economic and cultural backgrounds of students. Some education systems in this survey may be more efficient than others simply because of the quality of these contextual resources and largely irrelevant of their epistemological traditions.

A different kind of investigation might have produced answers which have eluded this present exploration. Two alternative approaches have attracted support. First is comparative pedagogy, where teacher classroom performance across national frontiers is evaluated. Efforts in this direction, especially in Britain, have been disappointing not only because of the difficulty of selecting samples of representative teaching which can be equated cross-nationally but, critically, because of the difficulty in selecting criteria of teacher effectiveness. The criteria adopted have been notoriously ethnocentric and the value of the results reduced accordingly.

The second approach also has been widely and justifiably criticized. This is the international comparison of outcomes, especially as measured by student achievement. The problems are similar to those in comparative pedagogy, of finding meaningful international indicators of achievement and of selecting comparable students to test across frontiers. Investigations of this kind have not been discouraged simply by methodological obstacles. Politicians' thirst for international comparisons of achievement is unquenchable and so problems of sampling and comparison are not accepted as unsurmountable barriers. It would be faint-hearted to dismiss all aspirations in this direction as utterly misconceived. Nevertheless, the present difficulties are too great for convincing investigations to be mounted with great confidence.

Conclusions: possibilities in England and Wales

What conclusions emerge from this present study with all its limitations? The Introduction promised a concern with the problems of English schools in adapting to a post-1992 Europe. The criticisms of English education have been severe. This is justified when English insularity has been associated with ideas of educational superiority which are not shaken easily. It is hoped that these criticisms have shown that other European countries have been at least as successful as England in meeting the problems of transmitting through systems of mass education knowledge appropriate to high-technology industrial societies. Furthermore these other countries have done it in ways that often differ sharply from those prevailing in England.

It is clear that all the countries of the European Community face difficulties in adjusting educationally to a single market Europe. Though England and Wales have especial difficulties in this respect, no country has adequately developed a system of inducing a level of rational thought, communication and action in the majority of its school leavers which is sufficiently high to meet the demands of a future high-technology society. Acquisition of rational knowledge should lead to rational action. It is a means to interrogate reality rather than to impose mechanically learned systems upon it. Rationality needs to be accessible to the whole population if it is not to be socially divisive and to create a non-rational underclass. Furthermore, each country faces almost unique obstacles to meeting the myriad of private knowledge demands which a Europe of culturally diverse nomads may generate. Some countries, such as France, are deficient in pluralist values. All are inexperienced in responding to the demands of migrant micro-communities.

Present difficulties in other European countries should not blind the English to the major weaknesses in their own education. Rational thinking is not encouraged in English educational objectives to the extent that occurs in the majority of European countries. This does put English youth at a serious disadvantage compared to their counterparts in other countries in the labour market if objectives to any degree correspond to outcomes. The English will need to learn to think logically and systematically if they are not to have the same kind of relationship with the rest of Europe than ancient Britain had with the Roman Empire.

Even the moderate ambition of sinking into genteel poverty in which humane rather than material values predominate may not be attainable unless it is recognized that English educational individualism is a very restricted phenomenon. Too often English students can only become the kind of individuals that teachers permit. Cultural diversity in nomadic Europe means above all consumer choice – that the recipients of education claim their individuality rather than having it thrust upon them. Only then can England claim genuinely to offer a more individualist education than other European countries.

What can be done? Certainly not to copy slavishly the practice of other European countries when successful transplants depend on the suitability of the soil of the recipient culture. England has a rational tradition which needs to be unearthed and made accessible to her educational clientele as a whole. It is the rationality of seventeenth-century England rather than of the twentieth-century French structuralists whose works mystified a generation of English university students of literature and sociology in the 1970s. Indeed, foreign inspiration may come as much from North America or the several cultures of Middle and Far East Asia, which each found its own way to be rational without recourse to Cartesianism.

A European dimension to English rationality and educational sub-culturalism will come inevitably as teachers, parents and children move across the continent and return with non-English values in their duty-free luggage. Educational producers and consumers both will find they have much to gain from trans-continental associations of interest. There is a need for an attitude of openness, curiosity and anticipation towards these links. In the end, each national educational culture may retain much of its own distinctiveness, which will add to the richness of Europe and to enhanced consumer choice. But distinctiveness will be accompanied by awareness of what rival cultures have to offer and by the universal acceptance of a minimum international currency of rational public knowledge.

Notes and References

Chapter One
1. For a summary and analysis of broad trends see, for instance, Gordon, D. M., 'The global economy: a new edifice or crumbling foundations?' *New Left Review*, 168, 1988, pp.27–30.
2. Gellner, Ernest, *Nations and Nationalism*, Oxford: Basil Blackwell, 1983, pp.114–122.
3. *Bildung und Wissenschaft*, 3–4, 1988, p.7.
4. *Bulletin of the European Communities*, 6, 1988, p.11
5. Straubhaar, Thomas 'International labour migration within a common market: some aspects of EC experience', *Journal of Common Market Studies*, 27(1), 1988, pp.45-58.
6. Neave, Guy, *The EEC and Education*, Stoke-on-Trent: Trentham Books, 1984, pp.10-11.
7. Ibid., p.15.
8. Neave, Guy, 'Cross-national collaboration in higher education', *Compare*, 18, 1, 1988, pp.53-61.
9. *Bulletin of the European Communities*, 6, 1988, p.11.
10. *Bulletin of the European Communities Supplement*, 10/73. 'For a Community Policy on Education 1973' (Janne Report).
11. *Bulletin of the European Communities*, 6, 1988, pp.10-11.
12. Giddens, Anthony, *The Class Structure of Advanced Societies*, London: Hutchinson 2nd ed. 1981, p.262.
13. Lukacs, Georg, *History and Class Consciousness*, London: Merlin Press, 1968. Marcuse, Herbert *One Dimensional Man*, London: Sphere Books, 1964. Adorno, Theodore, 'Cultural criticism and society' Connerton, Paul (ed.), *Critical Sociology*, Harmondsworth: Penguin, 1976, pp.258-276. Habermas, Jurgen, *Legitimation Crisis*, London: Heinemann, 1976.

14. Habermas, Jurgen, *The Theory of Communicative Action*, Vol.1, *Reason and the rationalization of society*, London: Heinemann, 1984, p.11.

15. See for instance Toffler, Alvin, *The Third Wave*, London: Collins, 1980.

16. Habermas, *Legitimation Crisis*, op.cit. Bell, Daniel, *The Coming of Post-Industrial Society*, New York: Basic Books, 1973. See also McLean, Martin, 'A world education crisis', *Compare*, 16(2), 1986, pp.203-210 for the educational implications of the distinction between 'technical' and private knowledge.

17. For speculation on the educational aspirations of modern European nomads see Tusquets, Juan, 'Increasing influence of nomadism on western culture and education', *Compare*, 11(2), 1981, pp.207-212.

18. Janne Report, op.cit.

19. Eliot, T.S., *Notes towards the definition of a culture*, London: Faber and Faber, 1948. Eliot was exploring territory mapped out previously by Matthew Arnold in *Culture and Anarchy* but reacted also to Karl Mannheim's sociology of knowledge and especially to *Man and Society*, 1944.

20. There has been some flirtation with the 'Basic School' in Spain and Portugal. See below pp. 57–8, 62.

21. See, for instance, Haigh, Anthony, *A Ministry of Education for Europe*, London: George Harrap, 1970. The Council of Europe work included the *European Curriculum Studies Project* (various authors), Strasbourg: 1.*Mathematics* (1968), 2.*Latin* (1969), 3.*Biology* (1970), 4. *Chemistry* (1972), 5.*Mother Tongue* (1972), 6.*Physics* (1972), 7.*Economics* (1972), 8.*History* (1972), 9.*Social and Civic Education* (1973), 10.*Geography* (1976). These dealt with the upper secondary school curriculum. A number of others in the 1980s focused on lower secondary and primary education, such as Council of Europe *Modern Languages*, Strasbourg, 1981.

Chapter Two

1. See, for instance, Wilkie Collins, *The Moonstone*, 1868:

> these puzzling shifts and transformations in Mr.Franklin were due to the effect on him of his foreign training. At an age when we are all of us most apt to take our colouring . . . he had been sent abroad and had passed from one nation to another, before there was any time for any one colouring more than another to settle itself on him firmly. As a consequence of this,

he had come back with so many different sides to his character, all more or less jarring with each other, that he seemed to pass his life in a state of perpetual contradiction. He could be a busy man, and a lazy man; cloudy in the head, and clear in the head, a model of determination, and a spectacle of helplessness, all together. He had his French side and his German side, and his Italian side – the original English foundation showing through every now and again.

Harmondsworth: Penguin, 1966, pp.76-77.

2. Madariaga, Salvador de, *Englishmen, Frenchmen, Spaniards*, London: Pitman Publishing, 2nd ed. 1970.

3. Lauwerys, Joseph A., Opening Address, *General education in a changing world*, Berlin: Max Planck Institute, 1965, pp.7-24. See also 'The Philosophical Approach to Education', *International Review of Education*, 5(3), 1959, pp.281-298.

4. Holmes, Brian, *Comparative education: some considerations in method*, London: Allen and Unwin, 1981. Bernstein, Basil, 'On the classification of education knowledge', *Class, Codes and Control*, Vol. 3, London: Routledge, 1977, pp.85-115. Becher, Tony, and Maclure, Stuart, *The Politics of Curriculum Change*, London: Hutchinson, 1978. Holmes, Brian and McLean, Martin, *The Curriculum: a comparative perspective*, London: Unwin Hyman, 1989.

5. The classificatory term naturalism is derived from J. J. Rousseau's distinction between man(woman) in nature and the citizen in the state. Rousseau, Jean-Jacques, *Émile*, London: Dent, 1911, p.7. Encyclopaedism and humanism are both citizen-orientated views of knowledge as they have been applied to the school curriculum.

6. An English observer in the first decade of the twentieth century suggested that French élite secondary schools compared to their English equivalents were 'much better for training boys of average or mediocre ability'. Brereton, Cloudsley, 'A comparison between French and English secondary schools', Board of Education, *Special Reports on Educational Subjects*, Vol.24, London: HMSO, 1911, p.300.

7. For an excellent yet sceptical historical analysis of French rationalism in its public, cultural and educational context in the late nineteenth and early twentieth centuries see Zeldin, Theodore, *France 1848-1945*, Vol. 2, Oxford: Clarendon Press, pp.205-242.

8. Durkheim, Émile, *The Evolution of Educational Thought*, London: Routledge and Kegan Paul, 1977, p.334.

9. *Ibid.*, p.335.

10. *Ibid.*, p.279.

11. *Ibid*, p.287.

12. Comenius, John Amos, *The Great Didactic*, London: Adam and Charles Black, 1907, p.70.

13. Most notably by Condorcet in his proposals to the National Assembly in 1792. See Barnard, H.C., *Education and the French Revolution*, Cambridge: Cambridge University Press, 1969, pp.81-95.

14. The encyclopaedic view in the USA, adopted after 1776, and as exhibited in the work of Benjamin Franklin, came to be dominated by the utility principle so that it was transformed into pragmatism.

15. Brereton, *op.cit.*, p.283.

16. Listed in *Le Monde de l'Education*, September 1988, pp.20-23 (my translations).

17. Hartog, P.J., 'The aim of the new curricula of French secondary schools for boys', Board of Education, *Special Reports on Educational Subjects*, Vol.24, London: HMSO, 1911, p.216.

18. *Ibid.*, p.212.

19. *Ibid.*, p.216.

20. Contained in Centre International d'Études Pedagogiques, *L'Enseignement en France*, mimeo, 1988, p.61 (my translation)

21. Fisher, H.A.L., *A History of Europe*, London: Collins, 1936, preface.

22. Hartog, *op.cit.*, p.221, Brereton, *op.cit.*, p.305.

23. Colomb, Jacques, 'France: development of mathematics teaching in French primary schools', Council of Europe, *Renewal of Mathematics Teaching in Primary Education*, Lille: Swets & Zeitlinger, 1985.

24. Brereton, *op.cit.*, p.298.

25. *Ibid.*

26. *Ibid.*, p.303, cf. the works of the 'Annales' school of historians in France and, later, those of Ferdinand Braudel.

27. See Hopper, Earl, 'A typology for the classification of educational systems', *Sociology*, 2, 1968, pp.29-46.

28. Durkheim, *op.cit.*

29. Bourdieu, Pierre, *Distinction*, London: Routledge and Kegan Paul, 1984, pp.4-5, 23, 69.

30. Horner, Wolfgang, 'The evolution of the notion of culture in the French pedagogical discussion', *Western European Education*, pp.62-80.

31. *Ibid.*, pp.67-69.

32. Herriot, quoted in *Ibid.*, p.70.
33. Hignett, Marcel F., 'The primacy of the rational in French secondary education', *Yearbook of Education 1958*, London: Evans Bros, 1958, p.235.
34. Quoted in Horner, *op.cit.*, p.72. Similar criticisms were made in the late nineteenth century. See Zeldin, *op.cit.*, pp.226-227.
35. Horner, *op.cit.*, pp.73-74.
36. Gramsci, Antonio, *Prison Notebooks*, London: Lawrence and Wishart, 1971, p.36.
37. *Ibid.*, p.35. See also School of Barbiana, *Letter to a Teacher*, Harmondsworth: Penguin, 1970.
38. Newcombe, Norman, *Europe at School*, London: Methuen, 1977, pp.26-27.
39. Gramsci, *op. cit.*, p.34.
40. *Ibid.*, pp.41-42.
41. Grudin, Robert, 'Humanism', *Encyclopaedia Britannica*, Vol.20, Chicago: Encyclopaedia Britannica Inc., 1988 15th. ed., p.723.
42. The content of secondary and higher education in Scotland in the nineteenth and twentieth centuries has been much more encyclopaedist in character, especially in the breadth of studies and in a rationalist perspective.
43. There is a considerable literature in this area. See, for instance, Wilkinson, Rupert, *The Prefects: British Leadership and the Public School Tradition*, London: Oxford University Press, 1964.
44. Plato, *The Republic*, Harmondsworth: Penguin, 1953, pp. 141-144, 156-173, 269-277, 282-283.
45. Bamford, T.W., *The Rise of the Public Schools*, London: Nelson, 1967, p. 118.
46. See Sampson, Anthony, *The Changing Anatomy of Modern Britain*, London: Hodder and Stoughton, 1982, pp. 240-259.
47. Plato, *op.cit.*, pp. 156-173.
48. In Plato's scheme, 'intelligence' was distinguished from and was seen to be at a higher level than 'reason'. By 'intelligence', Plato meant the innate capacity of the 'good' to perceive 'goodness', *ibid.*, pp.282, 283.
49. Locke, John, 'Some thoughts concerning education', in Axtell, James L., *The Educational Writings of John Locke*, Cambridge: Cambridge University Press, 1968, pp. 235-239.
50. Leavis, F.R. quoted in Walsh, William, *Uses of the Imagination: educational thought and the literary mind*. Harmondsworth: Penguin, 1966, p. 81.
51. *Ibid.* See also Mathieson Margaret, and Bernbaum Gerald, 'The

British disease: a British tradition', *British Journal of Educational Studies*, 28(2), 1988, pp.126-174.

52. For instance Weiner, Martin J., *English Culture and the Decline of the Industrial Spirit 1850-1980*, Harmondsworth: Penguin, 1985. Barnett, Corelli, *Audit of War: the illusion and reality of Britain as a great nation*, London: Macmillan, 1986.

53. James Joyce, *A Portrait of the Artist as a Young Man*. Harmondsworth: Penguin, 1960 p.215.

54. Board of Education, *Curriculum and Examinations in Secondary Schools* (Norwood Report), London: HMSO, 1943, pp.2-4.

55. Wilkinson, *op.cit.*, pp.125-230.

56. For a French educational humanist position on these points see Maritain Jacques, *Education at the Crossroads*, New Haven (Conn.): Yale University Press, 1966, pp.1-2, 5, 13, 15, 56-57, 66-69.

57. One of its better known champions was Robert Hutchins, President of the University of Chicago. See Hutchins, Robert M., *Education for Freedom*, Louisiana State University Press, 1943.

58. Dewey, John, *Democracy and Education*, New York: Macmillan, 1961, pp.88-91.

59. Lauwerys, 1965, *op. cit.*, p.15.

60. *Ibid.*

61. Ardagh, John, *Germany and the Germans*, Harmondsworth: Penguin, 1988, pp.226, 263-264.

62. In this way it was truer to the Platonic origins of humanism as a higher *stage* of knowledge appreciation, building on earlier developed reason. Plato, *op. cit.*, p.282.

63. Maclure, J.Stuart, *Educational Documents: England and Wales 1816-1968*, London: Methuen, pp.189-190.

64. The criticism of the Plowden Report in England suggested that it started from assumptions of biological growth and that the knowledge content was then arranged according to teachers' perception of this growth. See Bernstein, Basil, and Davies, Brian, 'Some sociological comments on Plowden', in Peters, Richard (ed.), *Perspectives on Plowden*, London: Routledge and Kegan Paul, 1969, pp.57-58 and Wilson, P.S., 'Plowden Children', in Dale, Roger et al., *Schooling and Capitalism*, London: Routledge and Kegan Paul, 1976, pp.158-162.

65. Bernbaum, Gerald, 'Countesthorpe College', in OECD/CERI, *Case Studies in Educational Innovation*, Vol.3, Paris: OECD, 1973, pp.7-88.

66. Max Planck Institute for Human Development and Education, *Between Élite and Mass Education: Education in the Federal Republic*

of Germany, Albany (N.Y.): State University of New York, 1983, p.138.

67. *Ibid.*, p.140.
68. Neiser, Bruno, 'Innovation in primary and secondary school education in France', *Western European Education*, 10(3), 1979, pp.33-36.
69. Kerschensteiner, Georg, *The Schools and the Nation*, London, Macmillan 1914. See also Simons, Diane, *Georg Kerschensteiner*, London: Methuen, 1966.

Chapter Three

1. State elementary education in France had expanded from the 1830s. It was only with the Ferry laws that a universal, free and obligatory system was applied. See Prost, Antoine, *L'Enseignement en France 1800-1967*, Paris: Armand Colin, 1968, which remains the most accessible and comprehensive history of nineteenth-century French education.
2. Prost argues that the Ferry laws replaced diversity by unification and an active, practical pedagogy by passive uniformity, *ibid.*, pp.276-282, 335-345.
3. See, for instance Weber, Eugene, *Peasants into Frenchmen: the modernization of rural France 1870-1914*, Stanford: Stanford University Press, 1976, and Thabaut, Roger, *Education and Change in a Village Community: Mazières-en-Gâtine 1848-1914*, London: Routledge and Kegan Paul, 1971.
4. The 1985 curriculum for the *lycée* specifies the kinds of occupations which students taking each specialism are likely to enter, even though the majority would spent three or four years in higher education first. Centre International d'Etudes Pedagogiques de Sèvres, *L'Enseignement en France*, Mimeo, 1986, pp. 62-63.
5. See Singer, Barnet, *Village Notables in Nineteenth Century France: Priests, Mayors, Schoolmasters*, Albany N.Y.: State University of New York Press, 1983.
6. *L'Enseignement in France*, *op.cit.*, p.55.
7. *Ibid.*
8. *Ibid.*
9. Freinet teachers were able to go their own way without too much interference. See Neiser, Bruno, 'Innovation in primary and secondary school education in France', *Western European Education*, 10(3) 1979, pp.33-36. In centralized systems, it is always possible to have different approaches which are isolated and thus sanitized by the description of 'pilot' project.

10. *L'Enseignement en France*, op.cit., p.15.
11. There are two types of vocational class for 14-16-year-olds – *classes pré-professionelles de niveau* (CPPN) and the *classes préparatoires à l'apprentissage* (CPA). The latter are for those who have already chosen an intended occupational field. These are 'sink' classes by official definition since the proportions of the age group in each are criteria used for designation of Priority Zones of Educational Failure in 1981 which could receive extra resources. Ministry of Education Information Service, *Primary and Secondary Education in France*, Paris: Ministry of Education, 1984, p.27.
12. Education Minister Alain Savary in 1981 encouraged inter-disciplinary school-level curriculum *projets d'action educatives* but they were linked to the Priority Zones. See below pp.50–1.
13. *L'Enseignement in France*, op. cit., p.58. The other two general aims were (i) to ensure mastery of the three forms of communication of writing, speech and pictorial representation and (ii) the develop-ment of the habit of personal work.
14. *Ibid.*, p.60.
15. However, mathematics for language or social science specialists is to be orientated to its applications in these fields, *ibid.*, p.63.
16. The other main aims were (i) the development of a 'culture' (ii) the expansion of the personalities of individual students so that they could make judgements (iii) the formation of responsible citizens, *ibid.*, p.62.
17. Neave, Guy, 'France' in Clark, Burton (ed.), *The School and the University: an international perspective*, Berkeley Calif.: University of California Press, 1985, p.25. There was a decline in the numbers in the letters branch and a rise in the relatively soft option G. (business studies) in the *baccalauréat de technicien*.

Baccalauréat Specialism	*Number of students*	
	1970	1983
A. Letters	64,500	45,180
B. Economics/Social Sciences	11,304	39,287
C. Mathematics/Physical Sciences	21,443	31,566
D. Mathematics/Biological Sciences	36,011	51,505
E. Mathematics/Technology	5,447	5,960
F. (B.Tn.) Technology	11,081	30,043
G. (B.Tn.) Business Studies	17,465	43,054
H. (B.Tn.) Information Science	54	701

(Adapted from Lewis, H.D., *The French Education System*, Beckenham Croom Helm, 1985, p.83.)

18. Much the same applied also to the older *brevet de technicien* which was a little more strictly vocational and was more likely to be terminal than the *baccalauréat professionel* but could still give entry to some kinds of technological higher education. The lower level two-grade *brevet d'études professionelles*, established in 1968, had a sufficient general education content for transfer to the *baccalauréat* to be possible and it had consequently a higher status.

19. Numbers passing the various examinations in 1983 were:

CAP	275,339
Baccalauréat	176,702
B.Tn.	75,130
Brevet E.P.	103,663

L'Enseignement en France, op.cit., annex 4.

The proportion of CAP students was much higher because the failure rate in the CAP (at about 60 per cent) was around double that of the other examinations.

20. Steedman, Hilary, 'Vocational education and manufacturing employment in Western Europe', in McLean, M. (ed), *Education in Cities: International Perspectives*, London: Institute of Education, 1989, p.54

21. There are also low-level general vocational courses often for low attainers with reduced job opportunities.

22. See, for instance, Stal, Isabelle, and Thom, Françoise, *Schools for Barbarians*, London: Claridge, 1988.

23. *Le Monde de l'Education*, December, 1988, pp.17-20.

24. See Pujol, Jacques, 'The lower secondary school in France: a note on the Haby reforms', *Compare*, 10 (2), 1980, pp.187-191.

25. *L'Enseignement en France, op.cit.*, pp.58-59.

26. This is not too difficult a jump to make in a society where French culture and universal culture are easily assumed to be synonymous.

27. See Stephens, Meic, *Linguistic Minorities in Western Europe*, Llandysul: Gomer Press, 1976, pp.369-384.

28. Around 16 per cent of school students in France are in private, mainly Catholic schools. After attacking church schools in the late nineteenth century, government had been surreptitiously increasing financial aid in the twentieth century. The law of 1959 dramatically expanded this aid so that almost all current expenditure could be offset by government if schools agreed to follow the

national curriculum, receive government inspectors and other conditions. Not all private schools accepted this arrangement.

29. For fuller details see Bourdoncle, Raymond, and Cros, Françoise, 'Teacher preparation and the reform of the colleges in France', in Tulasiewiez, Witold, and Adams, Anthony (eds), *Teachers' Expectations and Teaching Reality*, London: Routledge, 1989, pp.57-62.

30. There would also be out-of-school 'extra-curricular' activities (to use the British term) which in some instances would be student-run. French Ministry of Education, 1984, *op.cit.*, p.28.

31. Lewis, *op.cit.*, pp.48-51.

32. This phrase occurred in almost every official statement of educational purposes in the twentieth century. By the time of the 1975 Haby Law it had been modified from *the* culture to *a* culture. There was little elaboration of what this culture was. Implicitly it contained notions of a political loyalty to the institutions of national France as well as traditional concepts such as reason.

33. The problem of disruptive pupils, uncontrolled classes and vandalized buildings, previously associated with Britain and the USA, has grown in France. See Bourdoncle and Cros, *op.cit.*, pp.49-51.

34. Minio-Paluella, L., *Education in Fascist Italy*, London: Oxford University Press, 1946, pp.8-9.

35. *Ibid.*, p.40.

36. *Ibid.*, pp.88-89.

37. Borghi, Lamberto, 'Lower secondary education in Italy with particular reference to the curriculum', *Compare*, 10, 2, 1980, p.140.

38. 'Let's discuss the new curricula for the middle school', *Western European Education*, 13(1), Spring 1981, pp.10, 17.

39. *Ibid.*, pp.18, 33-35.

40. *Ibid.*, p.19. This kind of approach continues throughout the subject objectives – for instance History

    is intended to promote awareness of the past, to interpret the present and project the future by means of a basic awareness of important events at the political, institutional and socio-economic levels as well as at the specifically cultural level.
    Ibid., p.18.

41. Borghi, *op.cit.*, p.140. All other subjects (except religion, which is not tested) are examined orally within the school.

42. Elvin, Lionel (ed.), *The Educational Systems of the European Community: a guide*, Windsor: NFER/Nelson, 1981, p.167.

43. Holmes, Brian (ed.), *International Handbook of Education Systems, Volume 1. Europe and Canada*, Chichester: John Wiley and Sons, 1983, pp.450-452.
44. Elvin, *op.cit.*, p.88.
45. School of Barbiana, *Letter to a Teacher*, Harmondsworth: Penguin, 1970.
46. McNair, John M., *Education for a Changing Spain*, Manchester: Manchester University Press, 1984, pp.52-53.
47. In 1960 40 per cent of the labour force was in agriculture compared to 18 per cent in 1984. Organization of Economic Co-operation and Development, *Reviews of National Policies for Education: Spain*, Paris: OECD, 1986, p.10.
48. McNair, *op.cit.*, pp.56-57.
49. *Ibid.*, p.54.
50. Ministerio de Educación y Ciencia, *Proyecto para la reforma de la enseñanza: educación infantil, primaria, secundaria y profesional: Propuesta para debate*, Madrid: Centro de publicaciones del Ministerio de Educación y Ciencia, 1987, pp.73-74. Since this section was written, the Ministry of Education has produced a larger and more authoritative *Libro Blanco Para la Reforma de Sistema Educativo*, Madrid: Ministerio de Educacion y Ciencia, 1989. This document reaffirms the main elements of its predecessor of 1987. As yet it has not been translated into law.
51. *Proyecto para la reforma*, *op.cit.*, pp.83-84 (my translation).
52. McNair, *op.cit.*, p.63.
53. *Proyecto para la reforma*, *op.cit.*, pp. 117. See also note 50 above.
54. *Ibid.*, pp.115-116.
55. *Ibid.*, p.157.
56. OECD *Spain*, *op.cit.*, pp.22-24. Information on Galicia from Gina Romero-Vello.
57. OECD,*Reviews of National Policies for Education: Portugal*, Paris: OECD, 1984, pp.26-27.
58. Pires, Eurico Lemos, *Lei e Bases do Sistema Educativa: apresentaçao e comentarios*, Porto: Edicoes Asa, 1987, pp.114, 116.
59. *Ibid.*, p.114 (my translation).
60. *Ibid.*, p.117 (my translation).
61. van Daele, Henk, *Politics of Education in Belgium*, London: London Association of Comparative Educationists, 1982, p.21.
62. Dubreucq-Choprix, F.L., 'Decroly Method', *International Encyclopaedia of Education*, Vol 3, Oxford: Pergamon, 1985, pp.1335-1337.

63. Elvin, *op.cit.*, p.6.
64. *Ibid.*, p.9. In 1980, 93 per cent of 3-year-olds were enrolled.
65. Ministère de l'Education Nationale et de la Culture Française, *Faire le point sur l'enseignement secondaire renové*, Brussels: Ministère de l'Education et de la Culture Française, 1978, pp.99-100.
66. Elvin, *op.cit.*, pp.21-28.
67., *L'enseignement secondaire renové*, *op.cit.*, p.245.

Chapter Four

1. Arnold, Matthew, *Schools and Universities on the Continent*, Ann Arbor: University of Michigan Press, 1984, p. 197.
2. *Bildung und Wissenschaft* (hereafter *BW*) 10-11, 1984, p.144.
3. A frequently used descriptor which seems to have originated, in English, in Robinsohn, S.B. and Kuhlmann, J.C., 'Two decades of non-reform in West German Education', *Comparative Education Review* 11 (3), 1967, pp.311-330.
4. Mitter, Wolfgang, 'Curriculum issues in both Germanies: a comparative appraisal', *Compare*, 11(1), 1981, p.10.
5. *BW*, 3-4, 1982, p.48.
6. See Department of Education and Science (hereafter DES), *Education in the Federal Republic of Germany: aspects of curriculum and assessment*, London: HMSO, 1986, pp. 7-11, 16-23 for a fuller description.
7. Max Planck Institute for Human Development and Education, *Between Élite and Mass Education: Education in the Federal Republic of Germany*, Albany: State University of New York, 1983, p. 142. *BW*, 7-8, 1988, p.14.
8. *BW*, 6-7, 1986, p.19.
9. Newcombe, Norman, *Europe at School*, London: Methuen, p.9.
10. *BW*, 7, 1984, pp. 95-99.
11. Weiss, Manfred, and Mattern, Cornelia, 'Federal Republic of Germany: the situation and development of the private school system', in Walford, Geoffrey (ed.), *Private Schools in Ten Countries: policy and practice*, London: Routledge, 1989, pp.151-178.
12. Hearnden, Arthur, *Education, Culture and Politics in West Germany*, Oxford: Pergamon, 1976, pp.20-22.
13. Sadler, M.E., 'Problems in Prussian secondary education for boys', Education Department, *Special Reports in Educational Subjects*, Vol.3, London: HMSO, 1898, pp. 122-124.
14. *Ibid.*

15. Sadler, *op.cit.*, p. 87.
16. *Ibid*, p.89.
17. In the classical and modern language *Gymnasien*, students must follow English or Latin for all nine years; French, English or Latin for the last seven grades; and Greek or another modern language for the final five years. In the science *Gymnasien* English is studied in grades 5-10 and Latin or French in grades 7-10. This is reduced to English or French in grades 11-13 except for students transferring from the *Realschule* or *Hauptschule* who must take English and French until the end of the course. Max Planck, *op.cit.*, p.199.
18. *Ibid.*, p.197.
19. *Ibid.*, p.121.
20. *Ibid.*, p.212.
21. See DES, 1986, *op.cit.*, pp.11-15 for a full description.
22. *Ibid.*, p.6.
23. *BW*, 3-4, 1989, pp. 10-11.
24. Few *Realschulen* were established in Bavaria and they had a lower status than in north Germany. Max Planck, *op.cit.*, p.13.
25. *BW*, 6-7, 1986, p.19. The proportion of the age group taking the *Realschule* certificate is much higher since it includes 20–30 per cent of students in the *Gymnasium*.
26. *BW*, 5, 1986, p.10.
27. See Kledzik, Ulrich J., '*Arbeitslehre* – a new field in lower secondary education'. *Education Today*, 39(2), 1989, pp.9-17 for a brief but systematic description.
28. Prais, S.J. and Wagner, Karin, 'Schooling standards in England and Germany: some summary comparisons bearing on economic performance', *Compare*, 16(1), 1986, pp.30-35.
29. Mitter, Wolfgang, 'Education in the Federal Republic of Germany: the next decade', *Comparative Education* 16(3), 1980, p.259.
30. DES, 1986, *op. cit.*, p.22. This same point had been made 90 years earlier by Sadler, *op.cit.*, p.246.
31. DES, 1986, op. cit., p. 19.
32. There was a movement from a traditional study of grammar in the 1960s towards developing sets of rules for effective communication from an archetypical approach. It is claimed that new curriculum guidelines in the 1980s have undermined this by emphasizing simply language skills. Eroms, Hans-Werner, 'Teaching the mother tongue curriculum in Germany', in Tulasiewicz, Witold and Adams, Anthony (eds), *Teacher's Expectations and Teaching Reality*, London: Routledge, 1989, pp. 135, 138.

33. *BW*, 10, 1980, pp.115-116.
34. Max Planck, *op. cit.*, p.240.
35. Simons, Diane, *Georg Kerschensteiner*, London: Methuen, 1966, p.74.
36. *Ibid.*, pp.48-54, 65-67.
37. *BW*, 4, 1983, pp.64-66.
38. See Hearnden, *op.cit.*, pp.92-99 for fuller details.
39. *BW*, 5-6, 1987, pp.9–10, 12-13, 1987, p.13.
40. Mitter, 1980, *op.cit.*, pp.259-260.
41. *BW*, 5-6, 1983, pp.92-94, 7-8, 1983, pp.125-127.
42. *BW*, 8-9, 1980, pp.98-99.
43. Rist, Ray C., *Guestworkers in Germany: prospects for pluralism*, New York: Praeger, 1978, pp.206-222.
44. *BW*, 11-12, 1983, pp.177-179.
45. *BW*, 1-2, 1982, pp.16-17. Certain state schools recruit their pupils exclusively from one religious group so that it reflects and possibly cements a community culture.
46. Lijphart, A., *The Politics of Accommodation: pluralism and democracy in the Netherlands*, Berkeley: University of California Press, 1968.
47. Bagley, Christopher, *The Dutch Plural Society*, London: Oxford University Press, 1973.
48. DES, *Aspects of Primary Education in the Netherlands*, London: HMSO, 1987, p.23.
49. See Elvin, Lionel (ed.), *The Educational Systems of the European Community: a guide*, Windsor: NFER/Nelson, 1981, pp. 209-210 for details of secondary school organization.
50. DES, 1987, *op.cit.*, p.11.
51. Holmes, Brian (ed.), *op.cit.*, pp.512-513.
52. DES, 1987, *op. cit.*, pp.3-5.
53. Local authorities are also influential in curriculum matters. These elected bodies represent relatively small communities with an average population of fewer than 20,000 people.
54. Rordan, Thomas, *The Danish Folk High Schools* Copenhagen: Det Danske Selskab, 2nd ed. 1980, pp.13-23.
55. See Elvin, *op. cit.*, p.48.
56. *Ibid.* Only 6 per cent of all enrolments are in such 'small schools'.
57. For fuller details see DES, *Education in Denmark: aspects of the work of the folkeskole*, London: HMSO, 1989, pp.4-5.
58. Elvin, *op.cit.*, p.52.
59. *Ibid.*, p.58-59.

Chapter Five

1. Madariaga, Salvador de, *Englishment, Frenchmen, Spaniards*, London: Pitman Publishing, 2nd ed. 1970, pp. 51, 55.
2. *Ibid.*, p.55.
3. England has also 'borrowed' thinkers from the more studiously rational Scottish culture such as David Hume and Adam Smith. European *émigrés* have also had a role, in the twentieth century most notably Karl Popper, whose sceptical Cartesianism has been perceived as supporting a practical approach to inquiry, even though outside England it is seen as an important contribution to debate about the nature of a rational absolute knowledge.
4. Board of Education, *Report of the Schools Inquiry Commission* (Taunton Report), London: HMSO, 1868, pp.15-21.
5. Jackson, Brian, *Streaming: an education system in miniature*, London: Routledge, 1964.
6. While 'league tables' of international achievement in mathematics (which have to be treated with great caution) place English 13- and 14-year-olds below those of some other European countries, younger children do rather better. See Lynn, Richard, 'Mathematics teaching in Japan', in Greer, Brian, and Mulhern, Gerry (eds), *New Directions in Mathematics*, London: Routledge, 1989, pp.263-283.
7. From 1984 all new teachers have been required to have the equivalent of GCE 'O' level passes in English and mathematics.
8. Aldrich, Richard, 'A Common Countenance: national curriculum and testing in England and Wales', *Policy Explorations*, 4(1), 1989, pp.2-3.
9. Oxford and Cambridge had their own entrance and scholarship examinations which required similar specialization at an earlier date.
10. Unless national assessment at 16 is allowed to replace GCSE.
11. The British age participation rate in higher education at about 14 per cent is half or less than those of most other European Community countries.
12. Stenhouse, Lawrence, 'Some limitation on the use of objectives in curriculum research and planning', *Paedagogica Europae*, 6, 1970, pp.73-83.
13. The major projects were the Schools Mathematics Project and Nuffield Science Projects. See Flemming, Wilfred, 'The Schools Mathematics Project' in Stenhouse, Lawrence (ed.), *Curriculum Research and Development in Action*, London: Heinemann, 1980,

pp.25-41 and Walker, Rob, 'Nuffield Secondary Science', ibid., pp.79-93.

14. The inspectorate criticized the preponderance of pupils working endless examples in primary schools in the period 1982-8. DES, *Aspects of Primary Education: the teaching and learning of mathematics, a report by HMI*, London: HMSO, 1989.

15. It has been suggested, on the basis of empirical studies, that children who are successful in 'discovering' solutions to mathematical exercises and are highly regarded by their teachers have often a poor grasp of general mathematical rules, Johnson, David C. (ed.), *Children's Mathematical Framework 8-13*. Windsor: NFER, 1989.

16. DES, *Mathematics in the National Curriculum*, London: HMSO, 1989, especially pp.49-60. DES, *Science in the National Curriculum*, London: HMSO, 1989, especially pp.65-66.

17. In the English guidelines there had been a greater emphasis on understanding of linguistic structures and, particularly, the capacity to apply them. But these guidelines – which have been the object of the most intense public debate of all the subject prescriptions following the 1988 Act – remain all things to all men. Indeed they contain rationalist, humanist, pragmatic, nationalist, individualist and sub-cultural perspectives and are so overloaded that they almost invite teachers to do as they will with only a cursory nod to other approaches. In this area, the nature of assessment will be crucial. But, as in mathematics and science, there is no over-arching philosophy but simply a shopping list of 'targets' which lack coherence. DES, *English for Ages 5-11*. London: DES, 1988, especially pp.9-12, 15-16. Much was derived from an advisory report, DES, *A Report of the Committee of Inquiry into the Teaching of the English Language* (Kingman Report), London: HMSO, 1988, which recognized several perspectives on teaching English which were not reconciled. See especially pp.7-12.

18. For example DES, *The School Curriculum*, London: HMSO, 1981, p.14. The influential Cockcroft Report (DES, *Mathematics Counts*, London: HMSO, 1982) opened with a section entitled 'Why Teach Mathematics?' (pp.1-4) but it largely dismissed the argument that mathematics could develop logical thinking by claiming that this objective was the function of other subjects. Instead there was an emphasis on mathematics for its use in later life and as a means of communication.

19. See Papanoutsos, E.P., 'Educational Demoticism', *Comparative Education Review*, 22(1), 1978, pp.46-50.

20. Theodorakopoulos, I., quoted in Persianis, P.K., 'Values underlying the 1976–77 Educational Reform in Greece'. *Comparative Education Review*, 22(1), 1978, p. 54 (51-59).
21. Information from Amalia Ifanti.
22. Quoted in OECD, *Reviews of National Policies for Education: Greece*, Paris: OECD, 1982, p.79.
23. The national curriculum in the mid-1970s for secondary education was:

	Gymnasium (3 grades) (hours)	Lyceum (3 grades) (hours)
Classical Greek	17	22
Modern Greek	12	12
Mathematics	12	12
Sciences	13	10
History	9	9
Modern Languages	9	6
Religion	6	7
Geography	5	2
Physical Education	9	9
Latin	–	8
Philosophy	–	4
Music	3	1
Anthropology	1	1
Hygiene	1	1

(hours refer to the weekly totals over three grades). This curriculum is also compulsory for all students except in the last two grades of the *lyceum* where some subjects are studied by choice. Holmes (ed.), *International Handbook of Education Systems, Volume 1. Europe and Canada*, Chichester: John Wiley and Sons, 1983, p.353.
24. OECD, *Greece, op.cit.*, p.18.
25. *Ibid.*, p.19.
26. For the history of colonial and post-colonial education in Ireland see Coolahan, John, *Irish Education: history and structure*, Dublin: Institute of Public Administration, 1981.
27. *Ibid.*, pp.75-78.
28. Elvin, *op. cit.*, pp.135-136.
29. Quoted in Coolahan, *op.cit.*, p.54.
30. *Ibid.*, p.165.
31. *Ibid.*, p.207. A vocational subject can be substituted for history/

geography in vocational schools. The two other basic subjects can be chosen from a prescribed list.

32. *Ibid.*, pp. 208, 212. Within the Leaving Certificate examination course there are basic and more advanced courses.

33. The history of Scottish education may be followed in works such as Makie, J.D., *A History of Scotland*, Harmondsworth: Penguin, 1964, and Davie, George, *The Democratic Intellect: Scotland and her universities in the nineteenth century*, Edinburgh: Edinburgh University Press, 1950. Recent educational developments have been covered, comparatively, in Bell, Robert, and Grant, Nigel, *Patterns of Education in the British Isles*, London: George Allen and Unwin, 1977.

34. See, for instance, a number of papers in Bell, Robert, Fowler, Gerald, and Little, Ken (eds.), *Education in Great Britain and Ireland*, London: Routledge, 1973.

Bibliography

Adorno, Theodore, 'Cultural Criticism and Society', Connerton, Paul (ed.) *Critical Sociology*, Harmondsworth: Penguin, 1976, pp. 258–276.

Aldrich, Richard, 'A Common Countenance: national curriculum and testing in England and Wales', *Policy Explorations*, 4(1), 1989.

Ardagh, John, *Germany and the Germans*, Harmondsworth: Penguin, 1988.

Arnold, Matthew, *Schools and Universities on the Continent*, Ann Arbor: University of Michigan Press, 1984.

Bagley, Christopher, *The Dutch Plural Society*, London: Oxford University Press, 1973.

Bamford, T.W., *The Rise of the Public Schools*, London: Nelson, 1967.

Barnard, H.C., *Education and the French Revolution*, Cambridge; Cambridge University Press, 1969.

Barnett, Corelli, *Audit of War: the illusion and reality of Britain as a great nation*, London: Macmillan, 1986.

Becher, Tony and Maclure, Stuart, *The Politics of Curriculum Change*, London: Hutchinson, 1978.

Bell, Daniel, *The Coming of Post-Industrial Society*, New York: Basic Books, 1973.

Bell, Robert, Fowler, Gerald, and Little, Ken (eds), *Education in Great Britain and Ireland*, London: Routledge, 1973.

Bell, Robert and Grant, Nigel, *Patterns of Education in the British Isles*, London: George Allen and Unwin, 1977.

Bernbaum, Gerald, 'Countesthorpe College' in OECD/CERI, *Case Studies in Educational Innovation*, Vol. 3, Paris: OECD, 1973.

Bernstein, Basil, 'On the classification of education knowledge', in *Class, Codes and Control*, Vol. 3, London: Routledge, 1977, pp. 85–115.

Bernstein, Basil and Davies, Brian, 'Some sociological comments on Plowden' in Peters, Richard (ed.) *Perspectives on Plowden*, Routledge and Kegan Paul, 1969.

Board of Education, *Report of the Schools Inquiry Commission* (Taunton Report), London: HMSO, 1868.

Board of Education, *Curriculum and Examinations in Secondary Schools* (Norwood Report), London: HMSO, 1943.

Borghi, Lamberto, 'Lower secondary education in Italy with particular reference to the curriculum', *Compare*, 10(2), 1980, p. 140.

Bourdieu, Pierre, *Distinction*, London: Routledge and Kegan Paul, 1984.

Bourdoncle, Raymond and Cros, Françoise, 'Teacher preparation and the reform of the colleges in France', in Tulasiewiez, Witold and Adams, Anthony (eds), *Teachers' Expectations and Teaching Reality*, London: Routledge, 1989, pp. 57–62.

Brereton, Cloudsley, 'A comparison between French and English secondary schools', Board of Education, *Special Reports on Educational Subjects*, Vol. 24, London: HMSO, 1911.

Bulletin of the European Communities Supplement, 10/73. 'For a Community Policy on Education', 1973 (Janne Report).

Centre International d'Études Pedagogique, *L'Enseignement en France*, Sèvres, mimeo, 1988.

Colomb, Jacques, 'France: development of mathematics teaching in French primary schools', Council of Europe, *Renewal of Mathematics Teaching in Primary Education*, Lille: Swets & Zeitlinger, 1985.

Comenius, John Amos, *The Great Didactic*, London: Adam and Charles Black, 1907.

Coolahan, John, *Irish Education: history and structure*, Dublin: Institute of Public Administration, 1981.

Coombs, F.S. 'The politics of educational change in France', *Comparative Education Review*, 22(3), 1978, pp. 480–503.

Council of Europe, *European Curriculum Studies Project*, Strasbourg, 1.*Mathematics* (1968) 2.*Latin* (1969) 3.*Biology* (1970) 4.*Chemistry* (1972) 5.*Mother Tongue* (1972) 6.*Physics* (1972) 7.*Economics* (1972) 8.*History* (1972) 9.*Social and Civil Education* (1973) 10.*Geography* (1976).

Council of Europe, *Modern Languages*, Strasbourg, 1981.

Davie, George, *The Democratic Intellect: Scotland and her universities in the nineteenth century*, Edinburgh: Edinburgh University Press, 1950.

Department of Education and Science (hereafter DES), *The School Curriculum*, London: HMSO, 1981.

DES, *Mathematics Counts* (Cockcroft Report), London: HMSO, 1982.

DES, *Education in the Federal Republic of Germany: aspects of curriculum and assessment*, London: HMSO, 1986.

DES, *Aspects of Primary Education in the Netherlands*, London: HMSO, 1987.

DES, *English for ages 5-11*, London: HMSO, 1988.

DES, *A Report of the Committee of Inquiry into the Teaching of the English Language* (Kingman Report) London: HMSO, 1988.

DES, *Aspects of Primary Education: the teaching and learning of mathematics, a report by HMI*, London: HMSO, 1989.

DES, *Mathematics in the National Curriculum*, London: HMSO, 1989.

DES, *Science in the National Curriculum*, London: HMSO, 1989.

DES, *Education in Denmark: aspects of the work of the folkeskole*, London: HMSO, 1989.

Dewey, John, *Democracy and Education*, New York: Macmillan, 1961.

Dubreucq-Choprix, F.L. 'Decroly Method', *International Encyclopaedia of Education*, Vol. 3, Oxford: Pergamon, 1985, pp. 1336–1337.

Durkheim, Émile, *The Evolution of Educational Thought*, London: Routledge and Kegan Paul, 1977.

Eliot, T.S. *Notes towards the definition of a culture*, London: Faber and Faber, 1948.

Elvin, Kionel (ed.), *The Educational Systems of the European Community: a guide*: Windsor: NFER/Nelson, 1981.

Eroms, Hans-Werner, 'Teaching the mother tongue curriculum in Germany', in Tulasiewicz, Witold and Adams, Anthony (eds), *Teachers' Expectations and Teaching Reality*, London: Routledge, 1989.

Fisher, H.A.L., *A History of Europe*, London: Collins, 1936.

Flemming, Wilfred, 'The Schools Mathematics Project', in Stenhouse, Lawrence (ed.), *Curriculum Research and Development in Action*, London: Heinemann, 1980, pp. 25–41.

Fraser, W.R., *Reforms and Restraints in Modern French Education*, London: Routledge and Kegan Paul, 1971.

Gellner, Ernest, *Nations and Nationalism*, Oxford: Basil Blackwell, 1983.

Giddens, Anthony, *The Class Structure of Advanced Societies*, London: Hutchinson, 2nd ed., 1981.

Gordon, D.M., 'The Global Economy: a new edifice or crumbling foundations?', *New Left Review*, 168, 1988, pp. 27–30.

Gramsci, Antonio, *Prison Notebooks*: Lawrence and Wishart, 1971.

Grudin, Robert, 'Humanism', *Encyclopaedia Britannica* Vol. 20,

Chicago: Encyclopaedia Britannica Inc., 15th ed., 1988.

Habermas, Jurgen, *Legitimation Crisis*, London: Heinemann, 1976.

Habermas, Jurgen, *The Theory of Communicative Action*, Vol. 1, *Reason and the rationalization of society*, London: Heinemann, 1984.

Haigh, Anthony, *A Ministry of Education for Europe*, London: George Harrap, 1970.

Hartog, P.J., 'The aim of the new curricula of French secondary schools for boys', Board of Education, *Special Reports on Educational Subjects*, Vol. 24, London: HMSO, 1911.

Hearnden, Arthur, *Education, Culture and Politics in West Germany*, Oxford: Pergamon, 1976.

Hignett, Marcel F., 'The primacy of the rational in French secondary education', *Yearbook of Education 1958*, London: Evans Bros, 1958.

Holmes, Brian, *Comparative Education: some considerations in method*, London: Allen and Unwin, 1981.

Holmes, Brian (ed.), *International Handbook of Education Systems Volume 1. Europe and Canada*, Chichester: John Wiley and Sons, 1983.

Holmes, Brian and McLean, Martin, *The Curriculum: a comparative perspective*, London: Unwin Hyman, 1989.

Hopper, Earl, 'A typology for the classification of educational systems', *Sociology*, 2, 1968, pp. 29–46.

Horner, Wolfgang, 'The evolution of the notion of culture in the French pedagogical discussion', *Western European Education*, 12(2), 1980, pp. 62–80.

Hutchins, Robert M., *Education for Freedom*, Louisiana: State University Press, 1943.

Jackson, Brian, *Streaming: an education system in miniature*, London: Routledge, 1964.

Johnson, David C. (ed.) *Children's Mathematical Framework 8–13*, Windsor: NFER, 1989.

Kerschensteiner, Georg, *The Schools and the Nation*, London, Macmillan, 1914.

Kledzik, Ulrich J, '*Arbeitslehre* – a new field in lower secondary education', *Education Today*, 39(2), 1989, pp. 9–17.

Lauwerys, Joseph A., 'The Philosophical Approach to Education', *International Review of Education*, 5(3), 1959, pp. 281–298.

Lauwerys, Joseph A., 'Opening Address', *General Education in a Changing World*, Berlin: Max Planck Institute, 1965, pp. 7–24.

'Let's discuss the new curricula for the middle school', *Western*

European Education, 13(1), Spring, 1981.

Lewis, H.D., *The French Education System*, Beckenham: Croom Helm, 1985.

Lijphart, A., *The Politics of Accommodation: pluralism and democracy in the Netherlands*, Berkeley: University of California Press, 1968.

Locke, John, 'Some thoughts concerning education', in Axtell, James L., *The Educational Writings of John Locke*, Cambridge: Cambridge University Press, 1968.

Lukacs, Georg, *History and Class Consciousness*, London: Merlin Press, 1968.

Lynn, Richard, 'Mathematics teaching in Japan', Greer, Brian and Mulhern, Gerry (eds), in *New Directions in Mathematics Education*, London: Routledge, 1989, pp. 263–283.

Mackie, J.D., *A History of Scotland*, Harmondsworth: Penguin, 1964.

McLean, Martin, 'A world education crisis', *Compare*, 16(2), 1986, pp. 203–210.

Maclure, J. Stuart, *Educational Documents: England and Wales 1816–1968*, London: Methuen, 1968.

McNair, John M., *Education for a Changing Spain*, Manchester: Manchester University Press, 1984.

Madariaga, Salvador de, *Englishmen, Frenchmen, Spaniards*, London: Pitman Publishing, 2nd ed., 1970.

Marcuse, Herbert, *One Dimensional Man*, London: Sphere Books, 1964.

Maritain, Jacques, *Education at the Crossroads*, New Haven (Conn.): Yale University Press, 1966.

Mathieson, Margaret and Bernbaum, Gerald, 'The British disease: a British tradition', *British Journal of Educational Studies*, 28, 2, 1988, pp. 126–174.

Max Planck Institute for Human Development and Education, *Between Élite and Mass Education: Education in the Federal Republic of Germany*, Albany (N.Y.): State University of New York, 1983.

Minio-Paluella, L., *Education in Fascist Italy*, London: Oxford University Press, 1946.

Ministère de l'Education Nationale et de la Culture Française (Belgium), *Faire le point sur l'enseignement secondaire renové*, Brussels, Ministère de l'Education et de la Culture Française, 1978.

Ministerio de Educación y Ciencia (Spain), *Proyecto para la reforma de la ensenanza: educacion infantil, primaria, secundaria y profesional: Propuesto para debate*, Madrid Centro de publicaciones del Ministerio de Educación y Ciencia, 1987.

Ministerio de Educación y Ciencia (Spain), *Libro Blanco Para la Reforma de Sistema Educativo*, Madrid Ministerio de Educación y Ciencia, 1989.

Ministry of Education Information Service (France), *Primary and Secondary Education in France*, Paris Ministry of Education, 1984.

Mitter, Wolfgang, 'Education in the Federal Republic of Germany: the next decade', *Comparative Education*, 16(3), 1980.

Mitter, Wolfgang, 'Curriculum issues in both Germanies: a comparative appraisal', *Compare*, 11(1), 1981.

Neave, Guy, *The EEC and Education*, Stoke-on-Trent: Trentham Books, 1984.

Neave, Guy, 'France' in Clark, Burton (ed.) *The School and the University: an international perspective*, Berkeley Calif.: University of California Press, 1985.

Neave, Guy, 'Cross-national collaboration in higher education', *Compare*, 18, 1, 1988, pp. 53–61.

Neiser, Bruno, 'Innovation in primary and secondary school education in France', *Western European Education*, 10(3), 1979, pp. 33–36.

Newcombe, Norman, *Europe at School*, London: Methuen, 1977.

Organisation of Economic Cooperation and Development (hereafter OECD), *Reviews of National Policies for Education: Greece*, Paris, OECD, 1982.

OECD, *Portugal*, Paris, OECD, 1984.

OECD, *Spain*, Paris, OECD, 1986.

Papanoutsos, E.P., 'Educational Demoticism', *Comparative Education Review*, 22(1), 1978, pp. 46–50.

Persianis, P.K., 'Values underlying the 1976–1977 Educational Reform in Greece', *Comparative Education Review*, 22(1), 1978, pp. 51–59.

Pires, Eurico Lemos, *Lei e Bases do Sistema Educativa: apresentacao e comentarios*, Porto: Edicoes Asa, 1987.

Plato, *The Republic*, Harmondsworth: Penguin, 1953.

Prais, S.J. and Wagner, Karin, 'Schooling standards in England and Germany: some summary comparisons bearing on economic performance', *Compare*, 16(1), 1986, pp. 30–35.

Prost, Antoine, *L'Enseignement en France 1800–1967*, Paris: Armand Colin, 1968.

Pujol, Jacques, 'The lower secondary school in France: a note on the Haby reforms', *Compare*, 10(2), 1980, pp. 187–191.

Rist, Ray C., *Guestworkers in Germany: prospects for pluralism*, New York: Praeger, 1978.

Robinson, S.B. and Kuhlmann, J.C., 'Two decades of non-reform in West German Education', *Comparative Education Review*, 11(3), 1967, pp. 311–330.

Rordan, Thomas, *The Danish Folk High Schools*, Copenhagen: Det Danske Selskab, 2nd ed., 1980.

Rousseau, Jean-Jacques, *Émile*, London: Dent, 1911.

Sadler, M.E., 'Problems in Prussian secondary education for boys', Education Department, *Special Reports in Educational Subjects*, Vol. 3, London: HMSO, 1898.

Sampson, Anthony, *The Changing Anatomy of Modern Britain*, London: Hodder and Stoughton, 1982.

School of Barbiana, *Letter to a Teacher*, Harmondsworth: Penguin, 1970.

Simons, Diane, *Georg Kerschensteiner*, London: Methuen, 1966.

Singer, Barnet, *Village Notables in Nineteenth Century France: Priests, Mayors, Schoolmasters*, Albany N.Y.: State University of New York Press, 1983.

Stal, Isabelle and Thom, Françoise, *Schools for Barbarians*, London: Claridge, 1988.

Steedman, Hilary, 'Vocational education and manufacturing employment in Western Europe', in McLean, M. (ed.), *Education in Cities: International Perspectives*, London: Institute of Education, 1989.

Stenhouse, Lawrence, 'Some limitation on the use of objectives in curriculum research and planning', *Paedagogica Europae*, 6, 1970, pp. 73–83.

Stephens, Meic, *Linguistic Minorities in Western Europe*, Llandysul: Gomer Press, 1976.

Straubhaar, Thomas, 'International labour migration within a common market: some aspects of EC experience', *Journal of Common Market Studies*, 1988, pp. 45–58.

Thabaut, Roger, *Education and Change in a Village Community: Mazières-en-Gâtine 1848–1914*, London: Routledge and Kegan Paul, 1971.

Toffler, Alvin, *The Third Wave*, London: Collins, 1980.

Tusquets, Juan, 'Increasing influence of nomadism on western culture and education', *Compare*, 11(2), 1981, pp. 207–212.

van Daele, Henk, *Politics of Education in Belgium*, London: London Association of Comparative Educationists, 1982.

Walker, Rob, 'Nuffield Secondary Science', in Stenhouse, Lawrence (ed.), *Curriculum Research and Development in Action*, London:

Heinemann, 1980, pp. 79–93.

Walsh, William, *Uses of the Imagination: educational thought and the literary mind*, Harmondsworth: Penguin, 1966.

Weber, Eugene, *Peasants into Frenchmen: the modernization of rural France 1870–1914*, Stanford: Stanford University Press, 1976.

Weiner, Martin J., *English Culture and the Decline of the Industrial Spirit 1850–1980*, Harmondsworth: Penguin, 1985.

Weiss, Manfred and Mattern, Cornelia, 'Federal Republic of Germany: the situation and development of the private school system', in Walford, Geoffrey (ed.), *Private Schools in Ten Countries: policy and practice*, London: Routledge, 1989, pp. 151–178.

Wilkinson, Rupert, *The Prefects: British leadership and the public school tradition*, London: Oxford University Press, 1964.

Wilson, P.S., 'Plowden Children', in Dale, Roger et al., *Schooling and Capitalism*, London: Routledge and Kegan Paul, 1976.

Zeldin, Theodore, *France 1848–1945*, Vol. 2, Oxford: Clarendon Press, 1979.

Periodicals

Bildung und Wissenschaft (monthly), Bonn.
Bulletin of the European Communities (monthly), Brussels.
Le Monde de l'Education (monthly), Paris.

Index

Index of names